THE UNTOLD STORY

by

BISHOP EDGAR SHAW

1663 LIBERTY DRIVE, SUITE 200
BLOOMINGTON, INDIANA 47403
(800) 839-8640
www.authorhouse.com

© 2004 BISHOP EDGAR SHAW
All Rights Reserved.

No part of this book may be reproduced, stored in a retrieval system, or transmitted by any means without the written permission of the author.

First published by AuthorHouse 06/08/04

ISBN: 1-4184-6722-7 (sc)

This book is printed on acid-free paper.

Printed in the United States of America
Bloomington, Indiana

Drawings by Terry Brown and Robert Shabazz Smith

DEDICATION

I would like to thank God, His Son, and the Holy Spirit for giving me wisdom and knowledge, but most all, His Spirit.

Because of my development and relationship through Him, I dedicate this book to the Father, the Son, and the Holy Ghost. I take great honor and pride to be a descendant of the tribe of Judah, and having lineage of prophets in my family tree.

TABLE OF CONTENTS

FORWARD	ix
INTRODUCTION	xiii
Chapter 1 THE FIRST CONTINENT	1
Chapter 2 ADAM AND EVE IN THE LAND OF ETHIOPIA	9
Chapter 3 ENOCH THE CHOSEN ETHIOPIAN	13
Chapter 4 NOAH AND HIS SON HAM	35
Chapter 5 ABRAHAM THE RIGHTEOUS ONE	45
Chapter 6 THE HEBREW RACE	53
Chapter 7 MOSES AND ZIPPORAH	57
Chapter 8 THE SEPARATED AND THE ORIGINAL HEBREWS	63
Chapter 9 THE COMING OF THE LORD	67
Chapter 10 THE DOMINANCE OF THE EUROPEANS	73
Chapter 11 THERE'S NO BLACK OR WHITE	85
Chapter 12 THERE'S ONLY ONE RELIGION	93
Chapter 13 THE SCATTERED LOST TRIBES	109
Chapter 14 THE LAST PHARAOH	141
CONCLUSION	151

EPILOGUE 155
NOTES 157
LIST OF SOURCES 159

FORWARD

By Professor Hyacinth Ezeka, President
African Christian Fellowship, Baltimore (2000-2003)

The controversy of race and religion is an endless discussion and debate. However, when approached from the point of what God has said in the scriptures and what He has done for generations as Pastor Shaw has shown in this book, we then have our answer to the long debate. Pastor Shaw in this book is bringing a dimension not previously looked at by any scholars. It is very obvious that God has spoken in various ways concerning the Africans and the role that they will play in the end time ministry of the Lord Jesus Christ.

Starting from Genesis to Revelations, there are various references to groups as well as individuals, from different geographic areas that had played dominant roles to accomplish the plan of God here on earth. The roles played by these individuals and groups are sequential, coordinated and not random. These groups and individuals were not referred to by color rather they were referred to either by family linage, name or town. So when you read about Jesus of Nazareth, you know where He came from; or Abraham of Ur, or David the son of Jesse, you know which David and what his family linage is.

The essence of this book therefore, is to bring to light the mind of God concerning the group of people known as African or the black race in the plan of God. Scholars have argued for many years the exact physical locations of the Ethiopian referred to in the Book of Genesis and the exact location of the Garden of Eden. What is not controversial however, is the existence of Ethiopia in the continent of Africa. Also, the civilization that came out of the Empire of Ethiopia for thousands of years before Christ is never disputed. Well-documented body of literature and archeology exist today that the Empire of Ethiopia at one time encompassed the sub Saharan Africa, the North Africa, Middle East and portions of Asia including India.

Many have referred Africans as the custodians of God's secret plan for the world while the world sees Africans as a lost cause. To lead Israel out of Egypt, God prepared Moses as a boy and he, Moses labored for many years before his ministry started. His ministry was given a boost by the wisdom of an African priest named Jethro. The early years of Jesus Christ in Africa as a place of refuge where God has kept His secret plan for the world is well documented. In the salvation of mankind through the shedding of blood of Jesus, we see an African carrying the cross in fulfillment of God's plan to show the role that Africans should play in the entire plan of God. The Africans were part of God's initial plan to evangelize the world. In that, the Holy Spirit sent Philip to an Ethiopian eunuch, who later spread the gospel of Jesus to other parts of Africa. In essence, it will take Africans to evangelize Africa.

If you have traveled or paid attention to Christian news today, you will notice that Christianity is growing in leaps and bounds in Africa today, while on the decline in Europe and the United States of America. The Black Church in the United States has been the custodian of hope, the secret ingredient in the emancipation of the African Americans. All these are the plan of God as He prepares to end this wicked world for its sins.

Pastor Shaw has done mankind a great service in this book.

INTRODUCTION

Africa, the first continent that ever existed is mentioned in Genesis 2:13. Africa is where God first placed man and woman. Africa is also known for gold, aromatic resin, and onyx stone. Genesis 2:12 confirms that Africa today is the second largest continent that is three times larger than Europe. The population of Africa since 1988 is estimated 610 million. The earliest countries of Africa are Ethiopia, Egypt and Libya. These countries are mentioned in the Bible many times.

The **UNTOLD STORY** was given to me by God at least 20 years ago. He has compelled me to write this book. The purpose of this book is to shed light on a race that has been denied and misrepresented. I believe this book will help revive and strengthen a race of people who have been left out of the mainstream simply because of fear and jealousy. This book will bring about understanding to not only the Black race, but to others who need to be enlightened about where the first man settled and how man traveled from continent to continent until this current world today. The author's intent is to bring about a better understanding concerning the history of mankind and provide information on Jesus Christ, the Son of God and Enoch who was a prophet of God.

Chapter 1
THE FIRST CONTINENT

*In the beginning...*The Bible, which is the foundational book of which information for this book has been gathered depicts a history of chosen people who are people of color, and who also established civilization. According to Genesis 2:13, the first man, Adam, settled in the land of Ethiopia. Land and region are key components to where man lived. The Bible is not broken down by race, but by geography. In addition to land and region, lineage/ancestry and family stock is the second tool to where man lived.

The ancestry of the Black man begins with the Ethiopian who established Ethiopia and Egypt, countries in Africa, the first continent of the world. Cush, an Ethiopian, founded Ethiopia while his son Nimrod, founded Asia, the second continent. The Book of Genesis will show how man traveled from Ethiopia to Asia and later to Egypt.

BISHOP EDGAR SHAW

In the beginning...The ancient empire of Ethiopia was at one time remote, with the richest heritage in history. The Greeks considered Ethiopia to be the home of the gods and the retreat of the Muses. It was a land of fertile fields with riverbeds of diamonds and mountains of gold. Ethiopia was commonly considered the Isles of the Blessed. Also, Ethiopia was the land of the setting sun where the giant, Atlas, was compelled by the Olympian, Jove to prop up the heavens upon his head and shoulders. The Moors called the vast desert, which lies south of the Atlas, the Sahara.

The word, "Ethiopia" was originally pronounced "Aethiopia" meaning *sunburnt faces* (Ethiopia and the Missing Link in African History). Pliny, the Roman historian says the original Ethiopia was called Aetheria or Aeria. These names were derived from Aether, the son of the god, Valcan, which means "*heat*" (valcanised). Pliny says that the whole country of Africa was called Aetheria or Aeria and later Atlantia. The Greek writer concluded that the term "Atheria" meant Ethiopia while another Roman writer (Aulus Cellus) used the term Aeria for both Africa and Crete. Rome converted the term "Aeria" to the name "Africa" (Ethiopia and the Missing Link in African History). Many renown men in Roman history who had exercised heroic deeds in Africa were often surnamed Africanus. According to tradition, the wife of the giant, Atlas, was called Atheria. Tradition speaks that Atlas, the great king, founded the Atlantean Empire, whose enormous terrain ruled over two-thirds of the earth, including Africa, Asia, Europe, Mexico, Central and South America.

Both ancient and modern writers, including tradition, placed Ethiopia in Atlantis. The term Atlantis was the name of a continent or part of Africa according to Greek mythology and the ancient Egyptian records. Leo Frobenius, a scientist said that the Atlantis was part of Nigeria (western side) in the Yoruba country and the African Atlantis was the fragment survival. Colonel A. Brighane, in his book. The Shadow of the Atlantis" on page 214 says "Other ancient authors are even more explicit and associated Ethiopia with Atlantis."

The land of Ethiopia, which is also considered the seat of civilization, housed Adam and Eve, the first generation of mankind according to the Book of Genesis. Not only was Adam the first man, one could say he was the first king because he was in charge of the earth and every living thing on the earth. It is safe to say that Adam was a man of color having lived in the land of Ethiopia (Genesis 2:13).

In "The Sacred Annals", page 49 by Smith, a Hebrew commentator quotes, "Our Rabbis assert that Adam, our father of blessed memory composed a book of precepts which was delivered by God in Paradise." Ancient records now in possession of King Halie Selassie, says that Aram or Ori, the 35th son of Adam was the first king of Ethiopia. In "Josephus, History of the Jews", page 48, William Whiston says, "That there is an old tradition which says that Adam was the father of thirty-three sons and twenty- three daughters."

Over this vast span of time, much speculation has occurred concerning where man first settled. Evolutionists had theorized that man evolved from biological evolution. It must be acknowledged that man did not create himself, nor did he originate through evolution. Man came into being by virtue of a Supreme Being who created heaven and earth, and who positioned the moon and the stars in the firmament (Genesis 1). This particular Supreme Being was able to turn night into day, and create man and woman. Not only is it important to know where man started civilization, but it is also important to know the truth. The truth has not been taught simply because the adversary (Satan) has distorted the truth due to fear, jealously, greed and power.

This book will open your eyes to many things, but you must be willing to accept the truth. People have lived lies for centuries due to keeping the truth away. This book will demonstrate how the true people settled in Ethiopia and Mesopotamia.

It is recorded that God kept two copies of historic records and accounts. The first one dealt with revelation to man, which is the Bible. The other was destroyed- written remains written in a strange language of those lands from whence the Bible first came. Currently, man has access to the Bible.

THE UNTOLD STORY

Man, as we discovered, lived in the land of Ethiopia, which is the first continent of the world, as well as Asia. Historically, the Ethiopians were in the land of Mesopotamia, which is in the center of Babylon that is currently called Iraq. This civilization was in the southern part of Mesopotamia. There were two Ethiopian nations in ancient times, one on the eastern region of Africa, and the other was on the southern part of Asia. The people that migrated to the region were called Sumerians. They had established a number of cities in Asia. At that time, Ethiopians were not called "Ethiopians", they were named after the cities they lived in or conquered.

Hence, the Ethiopians were really the Sumerians who developed the first major civilization of ancient Near East called Sumer, which was later known as Babylonia. Ur, Erech, Accad, and Calneh were major cities of Sumer. Genesis10:8, "And Cush begat Nimrod", implies that Cush was Ethiopian. The name *Cush* means Ethiopia (Harper's Bible Dictionary). The inspired word of God points out that Cush's son, Nimrod, founded a number of cities. I recommend reading "From Babylon to Timbuktu" by Reverend Rudolph R. Windsor for more insight into the history and genealogy of Ethiopia.

Havilah was another son of Cush. The word *Havilah* in Genesis 2:11, became the name of a tribe and region known as the land of Havilah and the Havilites (Ethiopians) lived in the land of Havilah. Scholars have located this land near the Persian Gulf.

Race was never an issue as it is in our day. People that lived in a central area spoke one language; one part of the area was situated in Africa and the other in Asia, established by Ethiopians. Both Semitic and Hamitic language were the same language.

Ethiopians and Sumerians were related. The Sumerians founded cities that existed more than 4,000 years B.C., such as Eridu, Lagash, Nippur Kish, and Ur ("From Babylon to Timbuktu.) The damaged written remains refer to these cities.

Archeologists have found skeletons of ancient Dravidian and Nedda types in Ur and Kish (Webster's Dictionary). Gazetteer section says that Sumer is the Southern Division of ancient Babylon. Sumerian, the pre-Semitic population is of the lower Euphrates Valley. The pre-Semitic population means that the Black Sumerians were first or Ethiopians and their kindred appeared to have settled among the Mesopotamia to India. This area now includes Southern Iran, Afghanistan, Pakistan, and Northwest India.

The Chinese derived the blue print of their culture from a Chaldean who was a Kushite or of Ethiopian nature, the founders of Babylon Empire. Another reason for saying that the Chinese culture came from the Chaldee is because of such names as China, Chung King and Chang, which are similar, to Chaldee according to Professor Willis Broughton in "History of Ancient People". It says the inhabitants of China are of the yellow race type, but no doubt built upon a

Black foundation. The ethnologist found the evidence of remote pigmy or Negroid population (Pritchard in his "Natural History of Men", Page 237). The Aborigines (refer to Sterling M. Mecus, D. Hakin), of Cochin, China are called Mays and are people, which inhabit the chain of mountains, which separate it from Cambodia. They are a race of people very black and resemble the features of the Kaffir (South Africa) the Cochin-Chinese; they resemble them in their features and customs.

Indo-China anthropologists say there is some reason to believe that Southern China as then the Old Stone Age in Europe was occupied by Negroid or black curly haired pygmies that even exist in the Philippines, New Guinea and elsewhere.

Chinese culture, according to Dr. Charles Gutzlaff, in "History of China" was founded in 2205 B.C., according to the Bible. This would have occurred right after the dispersion, which was in Genesis 11:9. Refer to "Ethiopia and the Missing Link in African History" by D. Hakim.

Chapter 2
ADAM AND EVE IN THE LAND OF ETHIOPIA

The Bible reads that God made man (woman from the rib of man) and placed them — Adam and Eve — in a garden. A river went out of Eden to water the garden, and that river was parted and became four headwaters, Genesis 2:10-14. The name of the second river is called Gihon, which passes through the whole land of Ethiopia. From the location of this river, it implies that Adam and Eve lived in the land of Ethiopia. The third and fourth rivers center around Asia. These rivers confirm that man was situated in Africa and Asia due to the locations of the land and the rivers. Ethiopian chronologists say that Aram, the thirty-fifth son of Adam, ascended the throne of Ethiopia before Christ, 4,470 years, and twenty-one kings had ascended the throne before the flood. However, according to Ethiopian historians, there is another record of the long list of kings that was probably more accurate, but was carried to Egypt, when the Ethiopian kings ruled that country and was eventually destroyed when her power was overthrown.

In Genesis 2:7-14, following the creation of the first man, the Pishon River which compasseth "Havilah" (the area Havilah was located in Africa). It attained its name from the black man named Havilah who was the second son of Cush who founded Ethiopia, (Genesis 10:7), therefore making it affiliated to Adam's environment. The great Jewish historian, Flarius Josephus, a highly respected historian, offers keen respect of insight in this area. Josephus also acknowledged that the Gihon River which departed from Eden was the Nile River in Africa.

Biblical geography in this area of study revealed that the Pishon and Gihon Rivers at one time were associated with the Hiddekel and Euphrates Rivers prior to the Global Deluge. After a long period of time, there occurred a territorial change with the help of many volcanoes, floods, and earthquakes long after the great flood, which separated these rivers from Africa where Eden was located. The Greeks called the Nile, the River of Ham. Sepia Magazine published that Africa was the site of the Garden of Eden because of its vast resources and archaeological findings of the oldest prehistoric bones and artifacts in West and East Africa. Before man existed, God and His Son decided to make man in their image. (Genesis 1:26), "And God said, let us make a man in our image, after our likeness; and let them have dominion over the fish of the sea, and over the fowl of the air, and over every creeping thing that creeps upon the earth." Let's understand that God is a Spirit, and when He made man, He gave him a body, soul, and a spirit. Therefore, the first man, Adam and woman, Eve, looked like Him. Many contemporary Biblicists are in error by titling Adam and the Antediluvian people as Semitics (Hebrews or Jewish), (Japheth, Caucasian), (Hamitic, Blacks or Africans). Such name classification prior to the flood was non-instituted or unheard of, during the Antediluvian, before the flood). There existed neither Jew, African nor Caucasian by name. Instead, one people, having one regional language, living in proximity, and most certainly bare no other racial title than Adamics. The Lord God sent Adam out of the Garden of Eden to attend the ground from which he was taken. He drove out the man and placed Cherubim at the Garden of Eden with a flaming sword, which turned every way to safeguard the entrance to the tree of life. Adam lived to be nine hundred and thirty years old, and during that span he had sons and daughters who multiplied the earth until the days of Noah.

Chapter 3
ENOCH THE CHOSEN ETHIOPIAN

Enoch, who is mentioned in Genesis, Chapter 5:21-24, has very little said about him. However the history of the Ethiopians and the writings of this book confirm that he is Ethiopian. The Dead Sea Scrolls confirm that his writing is in Ethiopic language. He wrote the Book of Enoch and the Book of the Giants. All but one of the major components of the Ethiopic anthology has turned up among the scrolls. Enoch lived before the Flood during a time when the world was very different. Human beings lived much longer. Enoch's son, Methuselah, lived 969 years. One of the five books, entitled, "The Book of Jubilees," has survived and can be read in versions of Ethiopic and Greek. Among Ethiopian Christians, "The Book of Jubilees" was so treasured that it actually became a part of the Old Testament. Fifteen fragmentary exemplars of the Jubilees have turned up among the scrolls, establishing the work as one of the most common among those concealed landmarks, clearly testifying to its importance for those who hid the texts. Like the Ethiopian Christians, they may have considered the book as being the Bible.

According to the words of Enoch, in his manuscript, he starts out as saying, 'wherewith he blessed the elect'. During Enoch's time on earth, he saw visions dating back to Adam and Eve, and future visions like how man would be judged for sins in the world, and how the fallen angels were put away for their sins (Genesis 6:2 and II Peter 2:4). Now Enoch describes how the sin became so wicked before the sight of God, through the fallen angles. "The Book of the Giants" describes how two hundred angels lost their original estate, which was in heaven, by deciding to have children with human women. Through this change of events, their children became giants and grew 430 feet in stature. This caused the world to sin more. These giants dominated the world. The angels not only had intercourse with women, but with animals, therefore causing monstrous beings on the face of the earth. As the land became more wicked, the giants began to receive dreams, but could not interpret them. So, they asked Enoch to interpret them. The interpretation was that these giants would die in a flood, and that only one man, and his family would live through this flood. Due to the horrible sin on the earth, God translated Enoch to heaven.

THE UNTOLD STORY

Enoch also received visions, which he describes. In those days shall the elect and holy race descend from the upper heavens, and their seed shall then be with the sons of men. Enoch received books of indignation and wrath. Never shall they obtain mercy, saith the Lord of Spirits. He said a cloud then snatched him up, and the wind raised him above the surface of the earth, placing him at the extremity of the heavens. He said, I saw another vision; I saw the habitations and the couches of the saints. There my eyes beheld their habitations with the angels, and their couches with the holy ones. They were entreating, supplicating, and praying for the sons of men; while righteousness like water flowed before them, and mercy like dew was scattered over the earth. And thus shall it be with them forever and forever. At that time my eyes beheld the dwelling of the elect, of truth, faith, and righteousness.

Countless shall be the number of the holy and the elect in the presence of God forever and forever (Genesis 5:18-24). Jared lived one hundred and sixty-two years, and begot Enoch. After he begot Enoch, Jared lived eight hundred years, and had sons and daughters: and all the days of Jared were nine hundred sixty and two years; and he died. And Enoch lived sixty and five years and begot Methuselah: And Enoch walked with God after he begot Methuselah three hundred years, and begot sons and daughters: And all the days of Enoch were three hundred sixty and five years: And Enoch walked with God: and he was not; for God took him.

BISHOP EDGAR SHAW

Hebrews 11:5 confirms that, by faith Enoch was translated that he should not see death; and was not found, because God had translated him, for before his translation, he had this testimony, that he pleased God.

Richard Lawrence translated the manuscripts of Enoch from scrolls found in the caves of Ethiopia in 1773. These scrolls appear to be acquainted with the Dead Sea Scrolls, during that period. There is another author, named R.G. Charles, whose edition was published in 1912. Another discovery of seven fragmentary copies of Aramaic text have been discovered.

The Epistle of Jude 1:14-15, in the New Testament, confirms the revelations of Enoch which says, "And Enoch also, the seventh from Adam, prophesied of these saying, "Behold, the Lord cometh with ten thousands of his saints, to execute judgment upon all, and to convince all that are ungodly among them of all their ungodly deeds, which they have ungodly committed, and all their hard speeches which ungodly sinners have spoken against him." This epistle was written by Jude in A.D. 66, clearly signifying and confirming that Enoch's manuscripts did exist during this time.

There are confirmed studies that ten fragments of Enoch manuscripts found among the Dead Sea Scrolls. The famous scrolls only include a portion of the amount of findings at Qumran. Much of the balance was Enochian literature, including copies of the Book of Enoch and other apocryphal works in Enochian tradition, like the Book of the Jubilees. With numerous copies throughout, the Essenes could well have employed the Enochian writings as an organized prayer book or teacher's manual and study text.

The Book of Enoch was exercised by writers of then non-canonical, i.e. Apocryphal or hidden texts. The author of the apocryphal Epistle of Barnabas quotes the Book of Enoch three times, twice calling it "the Scripture", a term specifically denoting the inspired volume reflecting knowledge of Enoch's account of the Watchers, prominently the Testaments of the Twelve Patriarchs and the Book of Jubilees.

Many of the beginning church fathers also accepted the Enochian writings. Justin Martyr attributes all evil to demons whom he alleged to be the offspring of the angels who fell through lust for women (from the ibid) directly referencing the Enochian writings. Many other church fathers: Tatian (110-172); Irenaeus, Bishop of Lyons (115-185); Clement of Alexander (150-220); in addition to Methodius of Philippi, Minucius Felix, Commodianus, and Ambrose of Milanalso also approved of and stood behind the Enochian writings.

The twentieth century discovery of several Aramaic Enochian writings by J.T. Milik compiled a complete description of the Enochian writings, including translations of the Aramaic manuscripts. Milik's 400-page book, published in 1976 by Oxford (J.T. Milik, ed. and trans., The Book of Enoch: Aramaic Fragments of Qumran Cave 4, Oxford: Clarendon Press, 1976) is a milestone in Enochian scholarship, and Milik himself is no question one of the finest experts on the subject.

The Book of Enoch (also known as I Enoch) was one valued by Jews and Christians alike, until this book later fell in disfavor with powerful theologians, because of its controversial statements on the nature and deeds of the fallen angels. The Enochian writings, in addition to many other writings were eliminated (or lost) from the Bible. The Book of Tobit, Esdras, etc. were extensively acknowledged by many of the early church fathers as "apocryphal" writing. The Book of Enoch had been preserved by the Ethiopic church, which put it right alongside the other books of the Bible. Bruce obtained not one, but three Ethiopic copies of the book and brought them back to Europe and Britain.

Dr. Richard Lawrence, a Hebrew professor at Oxford, produced the first English translation of the work in 1821. It was then the modern world gained its first glance of the forbidden mysteries of Enoch. Most scholars would say that the present form of the story in the Book of Enoch was written sometime during the second book The earliest Ethiopic text was distinctly made from a Greek manuscript of the Book of Enoch, which itself was a copy of an earlier text. The original was clearly written in Semitic language, now thought to be Aramaic.

THE UNTOLD STORY

In spite of its unknown origins, Christians once accepted the words of this Book of Enoch as original scripture, considerably the part about the fallen angels and their prophesied judgment. In fact, many of the key concepts used by Jesus Christ himself seem directly connected to terms and views in the Book of Enoch. For an example, "And there came a voice out of the cloud, saying, 'This is my beloved Son', hear Him." But Luke's verse in the original Greek reads: 'This is my beloved Son, the Elect One (from the Greek Ho eklelegemenos, the elect one, hear Him". The *Elect One* is a most significant term (found fourteen times) in the Book of Enoch. Manuscripts of Enoch would be considered the most ancient part of the collection, dated back to the 3rd century B.C. Chapters 1-36. Excerpt below from "The Book of Enoch":

> Contemplation of the nature, descent of two hundred angels to earth - they took human women for their wives, begot children, (giants), Genesis, Chapter 6:2-4 led mankind astray but finally were destroyed by God. - Enoch's journeys in heaven, earth and underground.

> The words of Enoch, wherewith he blessed the elect and righteous, who will be living in the day of tribulation, when all the wicked and godless are to be removed. And he took up his parable and said, Enoch a righteous

man, whose eyes were opened by God, saw the vision of the Holy One in the heavens, which the angels showed me, and from them I heard everything, and from them I understood as I saw, but not for this generation, but for a remote one which is for to come. Concerning the elect I said, and took up my parable concerning them. The Holy Great One will come forth from His dwelling, and the eternal God will tread upon the earth, (even) on Mount Sinai, (and appear from His camp). And appear in the strength of His might from the heavens of heavens.

And all shall be smitten with fear and the Watchers (fallen angels) shall quake, and great fear and trembling shall seize them unto the ends of the earth. And the high mountains shall be shaken, and the high hills shall be made low, and shall melt like wax before the flame. And the earth shall be wholly rent in sunder. And all that is upon the earth shall perish, and there shall be judgment upon all men. But with the righteous He will make peace and will protect the elect, and mercy shall be upon them. And they shall all belong to God, and they shall be prospered, and they shall all be blessed. And He will help them all, and light shall appear unto them, and He will make peace with them.

Thousands of His holy ones to execute judgment upon all, and to destroy all the ungodly; and to convict all flesh of all works of their ungodliness which they have ungodly committed, and of all the hard things which ungodly sinners have spoken against Him.

Observe ye everything that takes place in the heaven, how they do not change their orbits, and the luminaries which are in the heaven, how they all rise and set in order each in its season, and transgress not against their appointed order. Behold, ye the earth, and give heed to the things which take place upon earth change, but all the works of God appear to you. Behold the summer and the winter, how the whole earth is filled with water, and cloud and dew and rain lie upon it.

Observe and see how (in the winter) all the trees seem as though they had withered and shed all their leaves, except fourteen trees, which do not lose their foliage but retain the old foliage from two to three years till the new one comes.

And again, observe ye the days of summer how the sun is above the earth over against it. And you seek shade and shelter by reason of the heat of the sun, and the earth also burns with growing heat, and so you cannot tread on the earth, or on a rock by reason of its heat.

Observe ye how the trees cover themselves with green leaves and bear fruit; wherefore give ye heed and know with regard to all His works, and recognize how He that liveth for ever hath made them so. And all His works go on thus from year to year forever, and all the tasks, which they accomplish.

But ye, ye have not been steadfast, nor done the commandments of the Lord, but ye have turned away and spoken proud and hard words with your impure mouths against His greatness. Oh, ye hard-hearted, ye shall find no peace. Therefore shall ye execrate your days, and the years of your life shall perish, and the years of your destruction shall be multiplied in eternal execration, and he shall find no mercy.

In those days ye shall make your names an eternal execration unto all the righteous, and by you shall all who curse, curse. And all the sinners and godless shall imprecate by you, and for you the godless there shall be a curse.

And all the…shall rejoice, and there shall be forgiveness of sins. And every mercy and peace and forbearance; there shall be salvation unto them, a goodly light. And for all of you sinners there shall be no salvation, but on you all shall abide a curse. But for the elect there shall be light and joy and peace, and they shall inherit the earth. And then there shall be bestowed upon the elect wisdom and they shall all live and never again sin, either through ungodliness or through pride; but they who are wise shall be humble.

And they shall not again transgress, nor shall they sin all the days of their life. Nor shall they die of (the divine) anger or wrath, but they shall complete the number of the days of their life. And their lives shall be increased in peace, and the years of their joy shall be multiplied, in eternal gladness and peace, all the days of their lives.

BISHOP EDGAR SHAW

And it came to pass when the children of men had multiplied that in those days were born unto them beautiful and comely daughters. And the angels, the children of heaven, saw and lusted after them, and said to one another, come let us choose us wives from among the children of men and beget us children. And Semjaza, who was their leader, said unto them, "I fear ye will not indeed agree to do this deed, and I alone shall have to pay the penalty of a great sin." And they all answered him and said, "Let us swear an oath, and all bind ourselves by mutual imprecations not to abandon this plan but to do this thing. Then sware they all together and bound themselves by mutual imprecation upon it. And they were in all two hundred, who descended in the days of Jared on the summit on Mount Hermon, because they had sworn and bound themselves by mutual imprecations upon it. And these are the names of their leaders:

Samlazaz, their leader, Araklba, Rameel, Kokablel, Tamlel, Ramlel, Danel, Ezeqeel, Baraqjal, Asael, Armaros, Batarel, Ananel, Zaqlel,

Samsapeel, Satarel, Turel, Jomjael, Sariel. These are the chiefs of tens.

And all the others together with them took unto themselves wives, and each chose for himself one, and they began to go in unto them, and defile themselves with them, and they taught them charms and enchantments, and the cutting of roots, and made them acquainted with plants. And they became pregnant, and they bare great giants, whose height was three thousand ells: who consumed all the acquisitions of men, and when men could no longer sustain them, the giants turned against them and devoured mankind. And they began to sin against birds, and beasts, and reptiles, and fish, and to devour one another's flesh, and drink the blood. Then the earth laid accusation against the lawless ones. And Azazel taught men to make swords and knives, and shields, and breastplates, and made known to them the metals of the earth and the art of working them, and bracelets and ornaments, and the use of antimony, and the beautifying of the eyelids, and all kinds of costly stones, and all colouring tinctures. And there arose much godlessness, and they committed fornication, and they were led astray, and became corrupt in all their ways. Semjaza taught enchantments, and root cuttings, Armaros the resolving of enchantments, Baraqijal (taught) astrology, Kokabel the constellations, Ezeqeel, the Knowledge of the clouds, Araqiel the signs of the earth, Shamsiel the signs of the sun, and Sariel the course of the moon. And as men perished, they cried, and their cry went up to heaven…And then Michael Uriel, Raphael, and Gabriel looked down from heaven and saw much blood being shed upon the earth, and all the lawlessness being wrought upon the earth. And they said one to another: The earth made without inhabitants cries the voice of their cryings up to the gates of heaven. And now to you, the holy one of heaven, the souls of men make their suit, saying, "Bring our cause before the Most High." And they said to the Lord of the ages, Lord of lords, God of gods, the King of kings, and God of the ages, the throne of Thy glory (standeth) unto all the generations of the ages, and Thy name holy and glorious and blessed unto all the ages. Thou hast made all things, and power over all things hast Thou; and all things are naked and open in Thy sight, and thou sees all things, and nothing can hide itself from Thee.

Thou sees what Azazel hath done, who hath taught all unrighteousness on earth and revealed the eternal secrets which were (preserved) in heaven, which men were striving to learn, and Semjaza, who whom Thou hast given authority to bear rule over his associates, and they have gone to the daughters of men upon the earth, and have slept with the women, and have defiled themselves, and revealed to them all kinds of sins. And the women have borne giants, and the whole earth has thereby been filled with blood and unrighteousness. And now, behold the souls of those who have died are crying and making their suit to the gates of heaven, and their lamentations have ascended: and cannot cease because of the lawless deeds which are wrought on the earth. And Thou knowest all things before they come to pass, Thou sees these things and Thou dost suffer them, and Thou dost not say to us what are we to do to them in regard to these.

Then said the Most High, the Holy and Great One spake, and sent Uriel to the son of Lamech, and said to him, Go to Noah and tell him in my name, "Hide thyself!" And reveal to him the end that is approaching, that the whole earth will be destroyed all that is on it. And now instruct him that he may escape and his seed may be preserved for all generations of the world. And again the Lord said to Raphael, "Bind Azazel and hand and foot, and cast him into the darkness; and make an opening in the desert, which is in Dudael, and cast him therein. And place upon him rough and jagged rocks, and cover him with darkness, and let him abide there forever, and cover his face that he may not see light. And on the day of the great judgment he shall cast into the fire, and heal the earth which the angels have corrupted, and proclaim the healing of the earth, that they may heal the plague, and that all the children of men may not perish.

Though all the secret things may the Watchers have disclosed and have taught their sons, and the whole earth has been corrupted through the works that were taught by Azazel; to him ascribe all sin." And to Gabriel said the Lord proceed against the bastards and the reprobates, and against the children of fornication; and destroy (the children of fornication and) the children of the Watchers from amongst men (and cause them to go forth; send them one against the other that they may destroy each other in battle; for length of days shall they not have. And no request that they (i.e., their fathers) make of thee shall be granted unto their fathers on their behalf; for they hope to live an eternal life, and that each one of them will live five hundred years. And the Lord said unto Michael; go, bind Semjaza and his associates who have united themselves with women so as to have defiled themselves with them in all their uncleanness. And when their sons have slain one another, and they have seen the destruction of their beloved ones, bind them fast for seventy generations in the valleys of the earth, till the day of their judgment and of their consummation, till the judgment that is forever and ever is consummated. In those days they shall be led off to abyss of fire; and to the torment and the prison in which they shall be confined forever. And whosoever shall be him; "Go to Noah and tell him in my name "Hide thyself!" and reveal to him the end that is approaching; that the whole earth will be destroyed, and a deluge is about to come upon the whole earth, and will destroy all that is on it. And now instruct him that he may escape and his seed may be preserved for all the generations of the world. And again the Lord said to Raphael; bind Azazel hand and foot, and cast him into the darkness; and make an opening in the desert.

And then shall all the righteousness escape, and shall live, till they beget thousands of children, and all the days of their youth and their old age shall they complete in peace.

And then shall the whole earth be tilled in righteousness, and shall all be planted with trees and the full of blessing. And all desirable trees shall be planted on it, and they shall plant vines on it; and the vine which they plant thereon shall yield wine in abundance, and as for all the seed which is sown thereon each measure (of it) shall bear a thousand, and each measure of olives shall yield ten presses of oil. And cleanse thou the earth from all oppression, and from all unrighteousness, and from all sin, and from godlessness; and all the uncleanness that is wrought upon the earth destroy from off the earth. And all the children of men shall become righteous and all nations shall offer adoration and shall praise Me, and all shall worship Me, and the earth shall be cleansed from all defilement, and from all sin, and from all punishment, and from all torment, and I will never again send (them) upon it from generation to generation and for ever.

And in those days I will open the store chambers of blessing which are in the heaven, so as to send them down upon the earth over the work and labour of the children of men. And truth and peace shall be associated together throughout all the days of the world and throughout all the generations of men.

Before these things Enoch was hidden, and no one of the children of men knew where he abode, and what had become of him. And his activities had to do with the Watchers, and his days were with the holy ones. And I Enoch was blessing the Lord of majesty and the King of the ages, and lo! The Watchers called me - Enoch the scribe and said to me, Enoch thou scribe of righteousness, go, declare to the Watchers of the heaven who have left the high heaven, the holy eternal place, and have defiled themselves with women, and have done as the children of the earth do, and have taken unto themselves wives: "ye have wrought great destruction on the earth. And ye shall have no peace nor forgiveness of sin; and inasmuch as they delight themselves in their children, the murder of their beloved one shall they see, and over the destruction of their children, shall they lament, and shall make supplication unto eternity, but mercy and peace shall ye not attain.

And Enoch went and said: Azazel, thou shalt have no peace, a severe sentence has gone forth against thee to put thee in bonds; and thou shalt not have toleration nor request granted to thee, because of the unrighteousness and sin which thou hast shown to men. Then I went and spoke to them all together, and they were all afraid, and fear and trembling seized them. And they besought me to draw up a petition for them that they might find forgiveness, and to read their petition in the presence of the Lord of heaven. For from then forward, they could not speak (with Him) nor lift up their eyes to heaven for shame of their sins for which they had been condemned. Then I wrote out their petition, and the prayer in regard to their spirits and their deeds individually and in regard to their requests that they should have forgiveness and length. And I went off and sat down at the waters of Dan, in the land of Dan, to the south of the west of Hermon: I read their petition till I fell asleep. And behold a dream came to me, and visions fell down upon me, and I saw visions of chastisement and a voice came bidding (me) to tell it to the sons of heaven, and reprimand them. And when I awoke, I came unto them, and they were all sitting gathered together, weeping in Abelsjail, with their face covered. And I recounted before them all the visions, which I had seen in sleep, and I began to speak the words of righteousness reproving the Watchers of heaven. These are the words of righteousness that reprove unrighteousness of the world, according to the Holy One of heaven and earth. I perceived in a vision speaking with a tongue of flesh, and with my mouth, which the Holy One put in the mouth of men, to speak to the loved ones of the world, who are to everlasting, and understand with the heart, as he created and given to men the understanding or comprehension, well he has given me the power of reproving the Watchers and its offspring of heaven. I have written your petition, and to my vision it has been shown me, that what your request will not be granted you as the world endures.

Judgment has been passed upon you, your request will not be granted. From this time forward, never shall you ascend into heaven; He has said that on the earth He will bind you, as long as the world endures, Jude 6.

But before these things you shall behold the destruction of your beloved sons, you shall not possess them, but they shall fall before you by the sword. Neither shall you entreat for them, not for yourselves. But you shall weep and supplicate in silence. The words of the book which I wrote.
(R.H. Charles)

Chapter 4
NOAH AND HIS SON HAM

Noah's second son Ham established a dynasty, which began 2,635 years B.C. The direct line of the Hamitic Dynasty lasted 650 years, and twenty-five kings are said to have reigned in succession during that period. The Bible does not state that Ham was the father of the Black race, however, Ham was a Black king and father of his country. The Black race had a background of twenty-five thousand years of culture before Ham ascended the throne according to pre-historic records dating back to the Stone Age. In addition, the name Cush, the sons of Ham, became a symbol of nationality and has been converted to mean Ethiopian or Negro. It appears that King Ham's reign was confined to the Continent of Africa, as the scriptures refer to Africa as the land of Ham.

It is important that we understand that none of Cain's seed went past the flood. Cain killed his brother Abel. Cain and his offspring were destroyed by the worldwide flood. After the flood, the generations of Noah, of the seed of Adam and Seth, would populate the world. Noah was the great grandson of Enoch, the Ethiopian, making him a black man. Noah was a righteous man who followed God's way. Enoch prophesied that Noah would build an ark in preparation of the flood. Noah was not only directed to foretell the approaching doom. He was also bidden to make preparations for avoiding it. With the desire and the determination that God gave, his purpose from God was to convince the world at that time to repent.

THE UNTOLD STORY

Therefore from God to Adam, to Seth and Noah, and his seed. Noah was five hundred years old and Noah begat Shem, Ham, and Japheth (Genesis 5:32).

> The earth also was corrupt before God, and the earth was filled with violence and God looked upon the earth, and behold, it was corrupt, for all flesh, for all flesh had corrupted His way upon the earth. And God said to Noah, the end of all flesh is come before us; for the earth is filled with violence through them; and behold, I will destroy them with the earth (Genesis 6:1-13). Only Noah and his wife, his three sons, and their wives were saved by entering the Ark. (Genesis 7:7 and 8:15-16,18)

When the Ark rested on the Mountains of Ararat, which is in the southeastern part of Turkey, extending into northwest Iran, and the people and state established there from the ninth through the early sixth centuries B.C., all human life was destroyed on the earth by the act of God, except for Noah, his wife, his three sons, Japheth, Shem, Ham, and their wives. They became the families that re-populated earth again. And God blessed Noah, and his sons, and said unto them, be fruitful and multiply, and replenish the earth (Genesis 9:11) The sons of Noah, Shem (Semite) and Ham (Hamite) and Japheth (Caucasian, Gentiles) and their wives were responsible for bringing forth the different races of human kind on the earth. Noah's two sons, Shem and Ham were Black. This likeness in skin color continued up until Gehaz, who was a black-skinned Semite but later fell under a curse by Elisha, which changed him as white as snow from Naaman's leprosy. Scripture says, the leprosy therefore of Naaman shall cleave unto thee, and unto they seed forever. And he went out from his presence a leper as white as snow (II Kings 5:27). That particular leprosy caused a change in Gehazi's genes and chromosomes. All of Gehazi's offspring, following his experience, took unto his likeness (white complexion). But before that incident, there were no white Semites by birth. Scripture also says in Leviticus 13:3 and the priest shall look on the plague in the skin of the flesh, and when the hair in the plague is turned white, and the plague in sight be deeper than the skin of the flesh, it is a plague of leprosy: and the priest shall look on him and pronounce him unclean.

It cannot be answered by scripture of what exact color Japheth was, but his descendants became white. The Bible confirms that his descendants were the Gentiles, Genesis Chapter 10:2-5. The generations of Japheth traveled to Europe. Ham, one of the sons of Noah according to Genesis 6:10, settled in Africa; and also sent many descendants into Asia where his seed established a nation. It is clear that Ham was a Black man. Ham is identified with Jupiter Ammon, and also Zeus, because both words were derived from a root meaning Black, dark, fervent, or sun burnt. The descendants of Ham led the way as pioneers in art, literature and science. Ham's sons are: Cush, which means Ethiopia, Mizrain (Egypt), Phut (Libya), and Canaan (Canaan).

The sons of Noah had re-populated the world (Genesis 10) which they and their descendants established nations. Genesis 11:1 says "and the whole earth was of one language, and of one speech." Genesis 11:4 says "and they said go let us build a city and tower whose top may reach unto heaven; and let us make a name, lest we be scattered abroad upon the face of the whole earth." It is clear in this scripture that the people in that time knew of God, and that their intentions was to aggravate. God speaks to His Son, 11:7, go to, let us go down, and there confound their language, that they may not understand one another's speech. Not only did the people understand one another's speech, they were scattered throughout the ancient world. This location was called Babel, which is in Asia. Noah's grandson Nimrod was a mighty hunter (Genesis 10:9) who founded cities Erech, Accad, Calah in the land of Shinar, also Asshur, and Nineveh, Genesis 10:8-11, Rehoboth, and Calah. Nimrod is the son of Cush, who founded Ethiopia. Nimrod's uncle (Mizraim) founded Egypt, therefore confirming their true blood relationship. During that time, the Ethiopians and Egyptians look closely alike. They're both under Ham's bloodline, which makes them Hamites.

Noah's sons Ham, Shem, Japheth, and their descendants, made up a total of 70 nations (Ham 30, Shem 26, Japheth 14). These descendants were called Hamites, Shemites, and Japhites. The Hamites were centralized in South Western Asia and North East Africa, Cush, the Upper Nile region, South of Egypt (Mizraim) Genesis 10:6 refer to (Harper's Bible Dictionary). Mizraim means Two Egypt - a reference to Upper (Southern and Lower Northern Egypt). Mizraim is the second son of Ham. His first son, Cush, who founded Ethiopia, his third son Phut, Libya, and his fourth son Canaan; the name of the city he founded is called Canaan, which is currently Israel today. All of the sons of Ham settled in Africa except Ham's youngest, Canaan, who lived in Asia. This confirms that color did not exist: one man one region, one nationality.

The Shemites include Shem's sons, Elam, Asshur, Arphaxed, Lud, and Aram. Elam the Elamites lived East of Mesopotamia, Asshur an early name for Assyria, in Northern Mesopotamia, which is mentioned in Genesis 2:14. Arphaxed, a form of Hebrew word for Chaldea which is Southern Mesopotamia. Lud, the Lydians of Asia Minor. Aram, located north, northeast of Canaan, which is known today as Syria.

The Japhethites, Japheth's sons lived generally north and west of Canaan in Eurasia Gomer. The people of Gomer (the later Cimmerians) and related nations lived near the Black Sea, Magog and Gomer, Madai, Javan Meshech, Tiras, Tubal, are the sons of Japheth (Genesis 10:2) refer to Harper's Bible Dictionary.

The Scythian people's region North of the Black Sea between the Carpathian mountains and the Den,

BISHOP EDGAR SHAW

inhibited by the Scythians 7th - 1st Centuries B.C. From the middle of the 4th century, the Sarmatians slowly superseded them. The Scythians produced ornaments and vases in gold and electrum with animal decorations although there were no surviving written work. Their spectacular archeological remains, including vast royal burial mounds which often contain horse skeletons. Gomer, the ancestor of a people from Southern Russia called Gimirrai by the Assyrians and Cimmerians. Javan, the fourth son of Japheth, whose descendants traveled to a region in Asia Minor. Isaiah 66:19, and Ezekiel 27:13 says Javan and Tubal are specifically referred to as coastlands, these scriptures are a confirmation that Javan and his brother are Gentiles. The Lord speaks to Isaiah, "and I will set a sign among them, and I will send those that escape of them unto the nations, to Tarshish, Pul, and Lud, that draw the bow, to Tubal, and Javan, to the isles afar off, that have not heard my fame, neither have seen my glory, and they shall declare my glory among the Gentiles. The Lord is saying for the task of Hebrews as God's servants, is to make His glory known to the Gentiles

Ezekiel 27:13 says, Javan, Tubal and Meshech, they were thy merchants, they traded the persons of men and vessels of brass in the market. The famous cities of Javan were Miletus, Ephesus, Smyrna (Rev. 2: 8-11) and Magnesia, a name for Greece overall, (Joel 3:6). The Greeks are truly the sons of Javan (Daniel 8:21). Javan also means Greece in Zechariah 9:13, Daniel 10:20 and 11:2.

BISHOP EDGAR SHAW

The survivors of the flood and their descendants built a tower that was made to reach Heaven. The tower was made of brick instead of stone; stone and mortar were used to build Canaan. There was very little stone available due to the archaeological discoveries. The typical Mesopotamia temple tower, known as Ziggurat, was square at the base and had sloping stepped side that led upward to a small shrine at the top, and reached to the Heavens. A similar ziggurat may be described in Genesis 28:12, other Mesopotamian ziggurats were given names demonstrating that they too were meant to serve as staircases from earth to heaven. The whole human race being led by Nimrod, Ham's grandson attempted to make history through rebellion against God. God then dispersed the people because of their rebellious pride. Refer to Harpers Bible Dictionary.

The word 'Babel' means, "getaway to a god". With God's calling of Abram out of the post Babel peoples, the story of God's ways with humankind shifts focus from universal history to the History of God's chosen people beginning with Abram and his descendants, that eventually paved the way for all to come under the Redemption which is salvation through Our Lord Jesus Christ.

Chapter 5
ABRAHAM THE RIGHTEOUS ONE

The Bible states in Genesis 10:1 that Noah had three sons, Shem, Ham, and Japheth, and their familial generations established the world, as we see it today. As I stated earlier, Ham and his descendants established Africa, which is the first continent and part of Asia. Shem and his descendants founded parts of Asia. Japheth's descendants founded Europe. It is clear that everyone was of the same color and language, until man attempted to build a tower to reach up to heaven (Genesis 11:4, 7-9). God eventually brought a child into the world, (Genesis 11:26), whose name was Abraham. Abraham was a descendant of Shem. Abraham, who is the father of many nations, also became the righteous one and the father of the Jewish race. Abraham traveled along with his father, Terah, brother Nahor, and wives from Ur of the Chaldeans, which is in Asia to the land of Canaan. I must point out that Abraham's family did not follow God's ways. The scripture says in Genesis Chapter 12:1, "Now the Lord had said unto Abram, get thee out of thy country, and from they father's house, unto a land that I will show thee. God had something specifically for Abraham, and his descendants, vs. 2 in the same chapter says, "And I will make of thee a great nation, and I will bless thee, and make thy name great and thou shalt be a blessing. It is clear that Abraham's family put their trust in other gods, not the supreme God. In Joshua, Chapter 24:2, God spoke to Joshua confirming Abraham's family, "And Joshua said unto all the people, thus saith the Lord God of Israel, Your fathers dwelt on the other side of the Flood in old time, even Terah, the father of Abraham, and the father of Nahor, and they served other gods. Verse 3 & 4 says in the same chapter, "And I took your father Abraham from the other side of the flood, and led him throughout all the land of Canaan and multiplied his seed, and gave him Isaac, and I gave Isaac Jacob and Esau, and I gave unto Esau Mount Seir, to possess it, but Jacob and his children went down into Egypt.

This land of Canaan that Abraham traveled to was given to him and his descendants by God, due to a curse placed on Canaan, Ham's youngest son. This curse occurred when Ham saw his father Noah drunk and naked, instead of Ham covering up his father, he went to notify his brothers of what he just witnessed, therefore causing Noah to curse his grandson Canaan.

THE UNTOLD STORY

The land that Canaan received was taken away from him and given to Shem and Japheth's descendants. Abraham was a descendant of Shem. God told Abraham in Genesis Chapter 12:1, "to leave his country". God's plan was to bless Abraham and his descendants, he said in Genesis, Chapter 12:2, and I will make of thee a great nation, and I will bless thee, and make thy name great, and thou shalt be a blessing. Abraham traveled to Asia Ur of the Chaldees. Ur, which is one of the oldest cities of the Southern Mesopotamia, also lies ten miles west of the Euphrates River. Its region during that time called the Chaldees which is at the head of the Persian Gulf, home to a loose confederation of (Semitic or Aramaic) speaking people organized along tribal lines. The Aramaic sections of the book of Daniel 12:5, 10: 4, 5:7 include Chaldeans among the learned magicians and conjurers. At that point in time Abraham became the father of the Hebrew race. God selected this man and his descendants to be His chosen people. Therefore He removed him from his homeland, and provided for him and his family a new land, which is called Canaan. It is clear that Abraham was a righteous man. God confirmed by saying in Genesis Chapter 17:4, "As for me, behold, My covenant is with thee, and thou shalt be a father of many nations. Remember, that Abraham's ancestor, Shem, Noah's son was a black man, and that Shem's brother Ham was black simply because of the region that Ham and Shem discovered. Also remember that Noah's great grandfather was a black man whose name was Enoch, and who was an Ethiopian. It is clear that through this lineage, that Abraham also was black and that the land given to him through the same lineage, which spoke the same language which is Semitic and Hamitic, confirmed that everyone was the same. This lineage confirmed the chosen people of God, that became the Hebrew race. It is also confirmed when you read Genesis Chapter 12:11,12. "And it came to pass, when he was come near to enter into Egypt, that he said unto Sarai his wife, behold now, I know that thou are a fair woman to look upon. Therefore, it shall come to pass, when the Egyptians shall see thee, that they shall say, this is his wife, and they shall kill me: but they will save thee which Abraham's purpose was to say to the Egyptians that Sarah was his sister, instead of saying his wife, they would have killed him if he would or she would agree to say that she was the wife." It is clear that history shows that Egypt is in Africa. Therefore the Egyptians, Abraham and his wife Sarah all looked the same. The difference between them was land or region. The King Melchizedek confirmed in Genesis Chapter 14:19, "and He blessed him, and said blessed be Abram of the Most High God, possessor of Heaven and earth". In Genesis Chapter 15:13-14, God confirms with Abraham how He will bless his descendants, but first they will be strangers in the land that is not theirs. And He said unto Abraham, know of a surety that thy seed shall be a stranger in a land that is not theirs and shall serve them, and they shall afflict them four hundred years. And also that nation, whom they shall serve, will I judge and afterward shall they come out with great substance.

The sons of Abraham by the Egyptian handmaiden of Sarah whose name was Hagar and God would bless

THE UNTOLD STORY

and multiply and make fruitful. He shall be the father of twelve princes and will make him a great nation. Ishmael is favored of God. Here is an illustration, the angel of the Lord who guarded Isaac (Gen. 22:11-13). Lot (Gen. 16:16-19-28) and Joseph (Gen 48:16) and protected Ishmael's mother in her pregnancy (Gen. 16:6-14) and then protected both Hagar and Ishmael (Gen. 21:15-21). These sources reiterate that God will make Ishmael a great nation (Gen. 21:18). But a great difference remains between the father and his son. Compare the favorable promise to Abraham (Gen. 12: 3) with the statement about Ishmael: his hand shall be against every man's hand and every man's hand against him (Gen. 16:12). According to the Elohistic source, Ishmael dwelt in the wilderness of Paran. This wilderness in Paran was the site where the Israelites camped after they left Mount Sinai (Num. 10:11-12, 12:16). The descendants of Ishmael in Gen. 25 had twelve sons, his second son Keder, whose name in Hebrew means dark, is a confederation of Arab tribes based in the north Arabian Desert.

In Gen. 25:13, and I Chron 1:29, The Kederites were a major force from the late eighth century B.C. and they also are mentioned in Assyrian and Neo-Babylonian sources. The seventh son, Massa, was an ancestor of a North Arabian tribe associated with Tema, his twelfth son, also was associated with an Arabian tribe. Let's now examine his second concubine wife, Keturah, who bore six sons and who settled to south and east of the Hebrews, with the descendants of Abraham. The first son Zimran, was also associated with Arabia, along the east shore of the Red Sea, west of Mecca called Zubran and his sixth son, Shuah, the meaning to an Assyrian term for an Aramaen land on the Euphrates or possibly a reference to an Arab or Armaen tribe inhabiting the upper Euphrates region. It is clear that Abraham's son was blessed wherever they traveled first from Israel to Arabia, and in Assyria along the Euphrates Region. The word of God said, he would be a father of many nations.

These nations that Abraham established through Ishmael's twelve sons, and his second concubine with Keturah, who had six sons, all discovered Arab countries. Prior to Abraham, Ham's grandson Seba, established Midian, which is currently Arabia today. Seba also was a black man. Keturah's fourth son, Midian, was named after the country Midian, Gen. 25:2. This land also became the land of Moses' wife Zipporah and his father-in-law Jethro, which also discloses the closely related Semitic and Hamitic languages and race, through Ham and Shem. This righteous man truly had faith in God. God tested Abraham by offering his son Isaac for a burnt offering upon one of the mountains, but as he was about to sacrifice his son, the angel of the Lord called and said, Abraham, and he said, lay not thine hand upon the lad, neither do thou anything unto him. For now, I know that thou fearest God, seeing thou hast not withhold thy son, thine only son from me.

Abraham lived a very old age after having Ishmael, whose mother was an Egyptian, a hand-maid servant. Sarah, his chosen wife from God, Isaac, who also was his chosen seed, and Keturah who became his concubine that had six children with Abraham. Genesis, Chapter 25:7 says, and those are the days of the years of Abraham's life which he lived, are hundred threescore and fifteen years. Then Abraham gave up the ghost and died in a good old age, an old man, and full of years, and was gathered to his people.

Chapter 6
THE HEBREW RACE

The Hebrew race descended from Ethiopia. Ancient Hebrew is a member of the Canaanite family of languages. Ham's youngest son, Canaan, established the Canaanite family, and his brother Cush, with the Cushites founded Ethiopia. It is clear that God decided to use this particular race of people to be his chosen people. Let us understand that man traveled from Ethiopia, which is in Africa, to Asia. And that Abraham's descendants are the Hebrew race. The chosen people, which is a religion, first occupied the land of Ethiopia (Genesis Chapter 2:13). At this particular time, no religion or chosen people were mentioned, until Abraham and his chosen seed. The people that lived in this region were Ethiopians named after their land. Their descendants founded other countries in Africa, Asia and Arabia. They also spoke the same language which was Semitic, Hamitic, and Aramaic, therefore making them the same race. It is proven that Noah's two sons Ham and Shem were black and that they are the great, great grandsons of Enoch the Ethiopian. Therefore, it sums up the Scripture which says in Amos, Chapter 9:7, "Are ye not as children of the Ethiopians unto me, O Children of Israel saith the Lord". When you read about Moses who was born in Egypt, you will know that Egypt is in Africa, confirming that the Egyptians and the Hebrews look the same, but their religion was not. The reason that they looked the same is because they came from the same family tree. Let's examine this point, when the king, (Pharaoh of Egypt) promulgated an edict to cast all the Hebrew male babies into the Nile River. Miriam and her mother hid the baby Moses in a basket. It would have been difficult to conceal him from her father's anger. In the period of Moses, the Black Egyptians enslaved Black Jews.

Another point to prove that the Jews were black is the leprosy laws, written in the 13th Chapter of Leviticus, and explained in the second chapter of the book. The strangest and most amazing phenomena concerning biblical leprosy was that the skin turned white. These laws of leprosy were given to the nation of Israel and they could not apply to a white nation. Herbert Wendt wrote in his book, "It All Began In Babel". All indications point to the fact that Asia was the cradle of the black voice. There is more than enough information that all the original Hebrews were black, even including the nations in the middle east, the Dravidians, who also were originally black people of India, the Cushites, who were Ethiopians, which inhabited the southern Mesopotamian Valley and that Abraham and Ishmael married African women (Egyptians). The Black Jews of India, Abyssinia (Ethiopia) and West Africa, considered themselves the original Jews because of the purity of their Israelite blood. This has been stated by Allen H. Godbey. The questions is how these black Hebrews became light in complexion. There were many invasions: 1) The Indo-European invasion or Germanic invasion of Asia; 2) The Greek invasion of the Middle East; 3) the Roman invasion of the Middle East and North Africa. And 4) the Jewish slave trade and the Arab slave trade. The Indo-European invaders penetrated the Middle East and mixed with Black Asiatics as far away as India during the second millennium B.C.

The European Scythians passed through Southern Russia and Central Asia as far as the borders of China. During the Greek and Roman invasion, their soldiers settled down in the Middle East and North Africa, they also married these people of color. The Jews at that time sold white slaves to the Arabs throughout Africa and Asia. The Black Moors from North Africa conquered Portugal and Spain, then transported thousands of white slaves of German descent to Africa. All of these white people who came or were brought to Africa and Asia were absorbed into the native population.

Chapter 7
MOSES AND ZIPPORAH

Moses, of the Levi Tribe, wrote many books than the five in the bible. Among the Dead Sea Scrolls, are nearly a dozen different works that do not appear in our bibles, but asset, by one device or another, that Moses was the author. Some of his works include: <u>The Jubilees</u>, <u>The Words of Moses</u>, and <u>The Test of a True Prophet</u>, and <u>The Temple Scroll</u>. Following are some of the words that Moses spoke:

> "Hear, O congregation of the Lord, and lend an ear, all who are here gathered bear witness to all his words and judgments. Cursed be the man who fails to preserve and carry out all the commandments of the Lord as spoken by Moses His anointed, and who fails to follow the Lord, the God of our Fathers, He who has commanded us from Mountain Sinai."

Zipporah, Moses' wife was from the land of Midian. Midian centers in modern-day Arabia. Seba who is Ham's grandson, therefore making Zipporah of African descent, founded Midian. The Bible confirms in Numbers 12, that Zipporah was an Ethiopian.

Zipporah who name means "beauty" was the daughter of a Midian priest called Jethro (Exodus Chapter 3:1). Now the priest at Midian had seven daughters and they came and drew water, and filled the troughs to water their father's flock. And the shepherds came and drove them away, but Moses stood up and helped them, and watered their flock. And when they came to receive their father, he said, 'How is that ye are come so soon today. And they said, an Egyptian delivered us out of the hand of the shepherd, and also drew water enough for us and watered the flock. And he said unto his daughters, and where is he? Why is it that ye have left the man? Call him that he may eat bread. And Moses was content to dwell with the man for he said I have been a stranger in a strange land. (Exodus, Chapter 2:16-21). Jethro and his daughters came from the land of Midian. The name Midian came from Abraham's concubine wife, Keturah, who had a son called Midian.

Moses and Zipporah's marriage endured, however, there were some harsh disagreements between them as it is often between mothers and fathers as it relates to the rearing of their children. Part of the disagreement was attributed to circumcision, to which Moses demanded.

THE UNTOLD STORY

But Zipporah, was not accustomed, however, she eventually accepted. Gershom and Eliezer were of mixed blood. Their mother's complexion was black, for she was a pure Ethiopian. And Moses was a dark-skinned Hebrew. The great Jewish historian, Flavius Josephus, who was an eyewitness of Jesus Christ, states that Moses had a Negro (Ethiopian) wife prior to Zipporah. Josephus gives details by saying, Moses, while living in Egypt as the general of the army, lead an invasion against Ethiopia. Following his conquest, the beautiful Thurbia, daughter of the Ethiopian king promised to marry him if he showed kindness toward her people, Moses vowed to this request.

God called Moses on the backside of the mountain of God, Horeb. Horeb was another name for Mount Sinai, traditionally located in the southwest part of the Sinai Peninsula. Moses experienced something powerful happening when God commanded him to put his hand into his bosom. Moses obeyed, and after with drawing his hand, discovered it to have turned leprous white. Then God commanded Moses to return his hand to his bosom. Moses did accordingly, and after withdrawing his hand for a second time found the snowy white hand to have changed to its original color, (Exodus 4:67).

It is clear that Moses was a man of color (African descent), and that he was in the land of Africa. Moses was at this time 80 years old. His life during the next 40 years was a part of the history of the Israelites. He died at the age of 120 years, and was not careful of his memory, leaving no monument of stone to mark his grave.

Biblical history describes the original Hebrew Rule enslavement for 430 years. God told Abraham in Genesis, Chapter 15, 13,14, that his seed would be a stranger in land that would not be theirs, and shall afflict them four hundred and thirty years. This nation became free, through the power of Moses, but they doubted Moses and God on many occasions. It occurred then they wandered in the wilderness for forty years, also they were scattered (Gen. 28:64), and the Lord shall scatter thee among all people, from the one end of the earth, even into the other, and there they shall serve other gods, which neither thou nor they fathers have known, even wood and stone. Joel 3:2, makes reference of a scattered race. I will also gather all nations and will bring them down into the valley of Jehoshaphat and will plead with them there, for my people and for my heritage. Israel, whom they have scattered among the nations and parted my land.

THE UNTOLD STORY

Chapter 8
THE SEPARATED AND THE ORIGINAL HEBREWS

The question is how did God separate the original Hebrews. Simply because his word said so, in Deuteronomy, Chapter 28:58-68. This scripture confirms the separation of the original Hebrews. "If thou wilt not observe to do all the words of this law that are written in this book, that thou mayest fear this glorious and fearful name, the Lord Thy God, then the Lord will make thy plagues wonderful, and the plagues of thy seed, even great plagues, and of long continuance".

It was clear to God that if any of his chosen people committed sin they would be punished, either through leprosy, wandering in the wilderness, or separation. God had proven himself many times through his power. First the separation of the Red Sea, dividing the water in dry land, drowning Pharaoh and his men in the

BISHOP EDGAR SHAW

Red Sea, presenting Manna (food) from Heaven, and the Ark of the Covenant, which they kept and protected them when facing their enemies. As you examine this separation these chosen people failed to live unto God's word, his commandments, therefore causing death, captivity and separation.

In the Book of Amos 9:7 God is speaking to the Israelites. "Are ye not as children of the Ethiopians unto me O children of Israel, said the Lord," meaning that they were first Ethiopian, originally living in the land of Ethiopia, now currently changed to Hebrew. This next scripture comes from Zechariah 9:13, confirming that Greece was preparing to invade the Black nation of Israel, led by Alexander the Great, who invaded Egypt in 332 B.C. This was the start pf European dominance for 2,300 years. Another invasion took place by the Roman Empire in 65 B.C., when armies under General Pompey captured Jerusalem. During this period, it was estimated 1,000,000 Jews fled into Africa, fleeing from Roman persecution and slavery. The slave markets were full of Black Jewish slaves.

One of the first prophecies revealed came when God spoke to Jeremiah saying, "I will call all the families of the kingdoms of the North, said the Lord, and they shall come and they shall set every one of his thrones at the entering gates of Jerusalem and all the wall there at round about and against all the cities of Judah (Jeremiah 1:15). God says, "He brought the children of Israel out of Egypt and blessed them but had eventually turned their backs on Him." He confirms it in Jeremiah, Chapter 2:7, "and I brought you into a plentiful country, to eat the fruit thereof, and the goodness thereof but when ye entered, ye defiled my land and made mine heritage an abomination". The second prophecy revealed came in Ezekiel, Chapter 5: 11 and 12. "Wherefore, and I live, saith the Lord, God surely because thou hast defiled my sanctuary with all thy detestable things, and with all their abominations, therefore will I also diminish thee, neither shall my eyes spare, neither will I have any pity".

The third part of thee shall die with the pestilence and with famine shall they be consumed in the midst of thee, and a third part shall fall by the sword about thee. I will scatter a third part into the winds and I will draw out a sword after them. Ezekiel Chapter 6:8, confirms of having a remnant yet will leave a remnant that ye may have some that shall escape the sword among the nations. When ye shall be scattered through the countries, God has spoken clearly that the original Hebrew race was scattered among the many nations of the world. These scattered people will remain in their countries until God and his Son returns.

Chapter 9
THE COMING OF THE LORD

Throughout this book, I have proven that man lived first in the land of Ethiopia, and that he traveled from Ethiopia, which is in Africa and then to Egypt, which is also in Africa. Let me point out to you that the descendants of Ham and Shem discovered Africa and Asia. Modern day Israel was founded by Ham's youngest son, Canaan, which the country was named after him during his time, located in Asia. Japheth's descendants are the Gentile's nation (Genesis 10:5), or European nations that did not emerge until about 3,000 years after the flood.

Ham's son, Phut founded Libya, which is in Africa. Ham's oldest son Cush, founded Ethiopia, and Ham's son Mizraim founded Egypt (Genesis 10:6). Ham's grandson Nimrod, founded Babylon, Ninevah, and

Assyria, which is in Asia. Genesis 2:14 confirms that Assyria is in the east of Assyria.

This early civilization that dates back to over 15,000 years is clear that the man was black, and that he clearly established civilization over 12,000 years through kings and dynasties. Genesis 1:26 states, "Then God said let us make man in our image after our likeness and let them have dominion over the fish of the sea and over the foul of the air; and over the cattle, and over all the earth and over every creeping thing that creepeth upon the earth." When God said, "Let us make man in our image…" he was speaking to his Son, Christ. Let us understand that God, the Father, the Son and the Holy Ghost are three. When he says image, He is himself and his Son's appearance. When he says, "Our likeness" that means of man being holy. You remember that the first man lived in the land of Ethiopia, Genesis 2:13. Well in Genesis 3:15, when man had fallen by disobedience, God decided to send a seed that would destroy Satan, meaning that God prepared his Son, Jesus Christ. Since God and his Son had an image of man, looking like the first man in the land of Ethiopia throughout the Old Testament man described in Africa, therefore, this will confirm that Jesus Christ is a Black man. Let me also say to you that three prophets describes how he looked in a vision, Daniel 7:9, 10:6, Revelation 1:14-15, and Ezekiel 1:26-28.

Flavius Josephus, former governor of Galilee who lived during the time of Jesus, said that Jesus was a

THE UNTOLD STORY

man of plain looks, extremely learned, full of vigor, with dark skin. Josephus went on to say that early Christians accepted this description of Jesus.

The date and birth of Jesus is not known, but the Bible teaches us that he came from out of the tribe of Judah, this tribe is considered to be the tribe that God had chosen. King David, who God selected as king to lead his people came from this same tribe. Jacob, who God gave twelve sons, his fourth son, Judah (Genesis 29:35) became the ancestor of this tribe. Jacob, who is the grandson of Abraham, confirms the lineage of Shem and Ham, who were black. We know that Jesus was born in Bethlehem, raised in Africa and Nazareth, descended from a Hamitic line, began his work in Cana and Capernaum, was born near Jerusalem, was crucified, and was resurrected on Sunday, the first day of the week. R. Eisler says that Jewish historian Josephus describes Christ as black-skinned with average features.

In the year 705 A.D., a gold coin of Jesus Christ and Emperor Justinium II, was circulated through Byzantine. The full face of Justinium showed him to have straight hair, no doubt there is no race besides the Black man that has wooly hair or one of a mixed race. There are people, who have said Jesus could not be black because of Him being Jewish or Hebrew during that time, in fact, it has nothing to do with color. Besides, genetic traits came largely through the cross-breeding due to the nations, with Babylon, Assyria, Greece, and Rome. Scripture says for they have taken

BISHOP EDGAR SHAW

our own daughter for themselves and for their sons so that thy holy seed have mingled themselves with the people of those lands yea the hand of the princes and rulers hath been chief in this trespass.

Ezra had been in Jerusalem, (Ezra, Chapter 8: 31) when the officials brought the problem of mixed marriages to his attention. Deuteronomy 7:3,4 says they were forbidden to marry anyone outside of their nation. There are people who believe today that Jesus comes from European descent, but history proves his African descent. The bible says in Matthew 27:32, Cyrene, is in Africa. A man named, Simon of Cyrene was the man who carried the cross of Jesus. Mary, the mother of Jesus was the black Madonna. According to the scripture, Mary was of the lineage of David and Solomon (Matthew Chapter 1, Luke Chapter 3:23-38) as seen in the genealogy of Jesus through his mother Mary. Roman Rolland, in his book, "If Christ and Mary were not Black", then why for centuries did all continents draw, paint and sculpture the two as blacks.

For centuries, people throughout Europe (Italy, France, Switzerland, Spain, etc.) in nearly every home and cathedral there had been paintings and sculptures of Mary with Christ as black, however, during the rise of white supremacy, and Napoleonic Empire, hundreds of thousands of black paintings and statues of Mary and Christ were mobbed or burned and replaced with white ones. Rupert the Benedictine nearly seven centuries before Napoleon, says that in his day paintings of Mary were dark and black. The only present European country that is still honoring the Black Madonna is Poland. Let me also say that the invasions of Ethiopia, which history proves mainly that their artifacts and paintings were stolen by European countries until this day. They are now trying to recover these items and their place in history.

When Pope Pius was head of the Vatican State, an official postage stamp was issued showing the Virgin Mary being a black woman. There was a similar stamp in Spain commemorating the black virgin and the child Jesus. M. Etude says that there were 230 black virgin shrines located throughout France and elsewhere.

A Washington Post article dated May 4, 1979, states that many of the earliest Madonnas were painted black until the Renaissance (Michelangelo 1475-1564) when it became popular to paint the Madonna (Mary) white. Mary, the mother of Jesus was a descendant of the interracial lineage through her father Heli, who was a descendant of the negress Rahuh, and her Jewish husband Salmon (Matt 2:5, Luke 3:23, 31-32).

Jesus Christ who has been portrayed by many people in different cultures, is truly described in God's word as a man who is returning to rapture his church (those that believe in him - all nationalities); but more importantly, His chosen people, that have struggled for many years through hardship, pain and long suffering and emptiness and now scattered throughout the world through their disobedience to God, He's coming back.

Chapter 10
THE DOMINANCE OF THE EUROPEANS

During the 10th century there emerged a kingdom that formed the basis of Abyssinia 1270. Although it remained independent throughout the period of European colonization of Africa, Abyssinia suffered civil unrest and several invasions during the 10th century, and was eventually reunited in 1889 under Menelik II with Italian support. In 1896, Menelik put down an invasion by Italy, which claimed he had agreed to make the country an Italian protectorate having partial control by a strong nation over a weaker power up to the period of the middle ages when it was divided into several semi-independent states governed by a fender system, which caused civil and eternal conflict. These conditions and her struggle for existence and independence externally seriously affected the progress of Ethiopia. She rebelled.

BISHOP EDGAR SHAW

The Mohammedan invasion with only the aid of five hundred Portuguese soldiers during the middle ages, she fought against the encroachment of the body's overwhelming odds, but she was and is still the lion of God and she has been able to survive the shock of fifty centuries after the fall of the Atlantean Empire which existed many thousands of years before the Flood. Freementius, the first Bishop was consecrated by Athanasius, the African Patriarch of Alexandria, Egypt. The National Church at Ethiopia is Orthodox Catholic the same as that of Greece. The Bible was first translated into the Ethiopian language (500 A.D.) There are eighty-one Books in the Bible, 46 Books in the Old Testament, and 35 in the New Testament. The picture of the Virgin Mary, the infant Savior, John the Baptist and the angels are painted black with wooly hair. Ethiopians were the same people that today we call Negroes. They were not white, nor yellow. They were black people, the direct ancestors of the African and American Negroes.

THE UNTOLD STORY

I must make light of the fact, that there's been much speculation today of where the Anti-Christ would be coming out of, either the East or West. Many scholars, teachers of numerous backgrounds have challenged this question. It appears no one has a definitive answer to this question. I believe to know God's word. It cannot be any bias to any particular group or race, and that person or group must show humility and obedience to God, and accept the truth. Due to having authority over someone, whether it may be politically or spiritually, people's thoughts become very cloudy causing that person not to know the truth, nor accepting it.

Following will demonstrate the forces or authority in control, which will confirm whether the Anti-Christ comes from the east or West, who Satan has used for centuries. Keep in mind, you must examine the east in its early civilization, until the powers of today, to determine the answer.

The Gentiles came from Noah's son, Japheth, whose descendants were the Europeans. Ham and Shem spoke Semitic and some of their offspring spoke Aramaic. This confirms the scripture when God spoke to Abraham in Genesis 17:5-7, "Neither shall thy name any more be called Abram, but thy name shall be Abraham; for a father of many nations have I made thee." The first nation began with Israel, Genesis 17:7-12. The second nation was among many nations through Ishmael, Genesis 17:20. The sons of Ishmael,

Genesis 25:13-16 settled in Arabia, Syria and as far east to Assyria.

During early civilization, the nations were all in the East, starting with Africa and Asia. In the beginning of this book, its been mentioned that Babylon, Media-Persia, which is currently Iran, where kingdoms oppose God's authority. The last of the strongest kingdoms was Babylon, 747-539 B.C. There, King Nebuchadnezzar 605-562 B.C., received a dream but could not interpret it. He called his magicians, and astrologers, and sorcerers (Daniel 2:1,2) and the Chaldeans to interpret the dream. None could interpret his dream. He then requested to see Daniel, who interpreted the dream and told him his kingdom would come to an end. In the dream, his kingdom was described as gold. The next kingdom in the dream, made of silver, the third kingdom was made of brass, and the fourth was made of iron, which was considered the strongest. The dream and prophesy are of the end times.

But now, it's time to shift to the European nations starting with Greece. The Book of Daniel was written around 605 B.C. This young man witnessed a number of visions from God. He saw the current kingdoms and future kingdoms, and finally the descending of God to remove them. Now I will begin to show you the start of the Gentile nation, Greece. The Books of Daniel and Zechariah first introduced the European (Gentiles) - Daniel 8:21,10:20, 11:2 and Zechariah 9:13 - Greece in fact is mentioned frequently in the New Testament, especially associated with the Apostle Paul. Paul

BISHOP EDGAR SHAW

writes to Thessalonica, a city in Macedonia, Philippi, and Corinth. Philippi was a city named after the Father of Alexander the Great. Paul also visited other cities in Greece (Acts 16:9-18, 2 Cor. 2:12).

Greece is a country, which lies at the central mountain structure of Southern Europe. Between 750-500 B.C. Greeks pushed for land, founded numerous colonies, the Aegean, along the Black Sea, in Cyernaica, Sicily, and Southern Italy as well as Asia Minor. The cities of Ephesus, Galatia, and Colosse were all situated in Asia Minor. Greece began its Dominance through Alexander the Great. Refer to Harper's Bible Dictionary.

Around 336 B.C., he invaded and conquered the Persian Empire, and numerous Greek colonies were established throughout the Near East to spread Greek culture and combine the two traditions. This was a result of force, causing change of dialect in which the New Testament was composed. This language was dominant until the sixth century A.D., through force and invasions.

After the death of Alexander the Great, four generals emerged to establish themselves kingdoms carved from his empire. Their names are: Ptolemy I in Egypt, Seleucus I in Western Asia, Lysimachus in Asia Minor, and Cassandra in Macedonia. Another king later derived from Seleucus I, his name was Antiochus IV Epiphanes 175-164 B.C. He conquered the East and Palestine, which became part of his kingdom. He

THE UNTOLD STORY

opposed the high priest, and God Himself. Antiochus dubbed himself Epiphases (meaning God Manifest). He halted sacrifices and desecrated the temple. The apostasy of Jerusalem's ruling priest in the second century B.C., prompted Antiochus's blasphemous actions. The temple was in desecration for nearly seven years (2,300 days). Antiochus persecuted the land, the Jews, and the temple. The time persecution would continue. Antiochus was a cunning and deceitful king and his battle continued against the Jews and God until he died of an unknown sickness.

Rome eventually colonized Greece around 148 B.C. The Roman Empire spread over to the Mediterranean Sea and in Europe. The events in the Old Testament took place before the emergence of Rome. Rome's effect extended from mid-third century B.C. through early second century A.D. The Romans expanded their power outside of Italy. Sicily came under Roman control 241 B.C., which was first occupied by Greece. Sardinia in 231 B.C. Spain was added 201 B.C., which took two centuries to complete. Refer to Harper's Bible Dictionary.

In the year 146 B.C., the destruction of Carthage (North Africa) and its general, Hannibal, who in exile had finally lost its territory and became a Roman Province, this became a wave of dominance throughout the East.

The Roman Emperors during their reign:

Augustus	27 B.C. - 117 A.D.
Tiberius	14-37 A.D.
Caligula	37-41
Claudius	41-54
Nero	54-68
Galba	68-69
Vespasian	69-79
Titus	79-81
Domitianus	81-96
Nera	96-98
Trajan	98-117

The title that they held was called "Caesar", named after Julius Caesar.

The first Emperor, Augustus, who was the grandnephew and adopted heir of Julius Caesar, who was confirmed by the Roman Senate in 27 B.C. He was the Roman ruler when Jesus Christ was born in the Roman Province of Judea (Luke 2:1). Though Augustus was in fact the sole ruler of the Empire, he outwardly satisfied himself with only the necessary powers of rule, the supreme command of most of the army and the consular powers over the city of Rome. When Augustus ceased to stand for annual election to the consulate, he was granted new tribunician powers. These included powers he already possessed, such as personal immunity from persecution. He added powers to convene the Senate and popular assembly, and to submit measures to either at any time. He could also veto any item of public business or the action of any other magistrate. Administration of provinces requiring

THE UNTOLD STORY

military presence was entrusted to legates who were personal emissaries of the Emperor. Augustus created the foundations of Roman imperial power. As the title, Caesar, Augustus that was derived from a word associated with sanctuaries, suggests he initiated the process, which identified the Emperor and his family with the majesty of the Roman State and in later times, a deified.

These Emperors showed consistent rulership over the course of time:

Julius Gaius Caesar 100-44 B.C. - A Roman general and author, who conquered Gaul 58-51 B.C. and the civil wars of 49-45 B.C., and invaded Britain 55-54 B.C. He dispersed the supporters of his rival Pompey and the Roman Senate and emerged a dictator. He was assassinated March 15, 44 B.C.

Caligula Gaius 12-41 A.D. Roman Emperor, son of Germanicus and successor to Tiberius 37 A.D. Caligula was a cruel tyrant and was assassinated by an officer of his guard. Believed to have been mentally unstable, he is remembered for giving a consulship to his horse Incitatus.

Claudius Tiberius, the fourth Roman Emperor 10 B.C.-55 A.D., made Roman Emperor by his troops in 41 A.D., after the murder of his nephew Caligula. Claudius was a scholar historian and able administrator. During his reign, the Roman Empire was considerably extended, and in 43 A.D. he took part in the invasion of Britain. Lame and suffering from a speech impediment, he was frequently the object of ridicule. He was dominated by his third wife, Messalina whom he ultimately had executed, and is thought to have been poisoned by his fourth wife, Agrippina.

Nero, 37-68 A.D., Roman Emperor from 54. He is said to have murdered his stepfather Claudius' son Britannicus, his mother, his wives Octavia and Poppaea and many others. After the great fire in Rome 64 A.D., he presented the Christians, who were suspected of causing it. Military revolt followed 68, the Senate condemned Nero to death, and he committed suicide. Nero was adopted by Claudius, and succeeded him as Emperor in 54. (Webster New World Encyclopedia)

Titus Flavius Domitianus 51-96 A.D. Roman Emperor from 81. He finalized the conquest of Britain, suppressed immorality as well as freedom of thought in philosophy and religion. He persecuted the Christians. His reign of hatred eventually lead him to be assassinated.

When mentioning the Eastern Kingdoms and where would the Anti-Christ come from outside of, either the East or the West. This last kingdom of the four in Rome, had incredible military might, which Daniel confirms of its strength (Daniel 2:40). And the fourth kingdom shall be strong as iron: Understand the kingdom's names are not mentioned, but only their strength. Remember you must clearly know history to understand God's word, simply because His word was given to His chosen people to follow, and to warn of the consequences even if it cost them to be enslaved.

Rome transformed the various parts of its empire into an enormous military machine, combining strength with an efficient police and judicial system. Rome ruled the world longer than any of the three. The Roman Empire split into two portions after the rule of Emperor Constantine around 330 A.D.

The Revived Roman Government

The last part of that dream concerned the final stage of the world's empires represented by the ten toes of iron and clay, which means the Roman Empire consisting of ten nations united in a confederacy. Since Israel's rebirth as a nation in 1948, Europe has begun to come together more as a United Federation for economic trade and security reasons. In 1992, European nations gathered to discuss future moves toward full integration of member economics utilizing one economic system, a common monetary system as well as a common defense capability and foreign policy. Today, fifteen member states belong to the European Union, creating one of the largest economic political and military powers in the western world.

Daniel prophesied about a united federation under the revived Roman Empire, which represents these ten toes or nations (Daniel 2:42, Rev 13). Today, this revived government dominates the world as did Rome.

Chapter 11
THERE'S NO BLACK OR WHITE

I have proven that man came from out of Ethiopia (Africa) Genesis 2:13, and that have traveled to the Southern part of Asia, which is called Mesopotamia (Genesis 2:14). The Ethiopians are not described by color, but by regions. The descendants who came after them were all Ethiopians beginning with Adam until Noah and his family. Noah as you recall, was the great grandson of Enoch.

Noah's three sons were all the same, Ham, Shem and Japheth. The color of a man never occurred until the Leprosy Laws. On many occasions this was due to disobedience of God's chosen people. When God called Moses, he demonstrated in a form of a miracle of having Moses place his hand on his bosom; after placing his hand it became white as snow. He then returned his hand it became normal flesh. (Exodus 4:

BISHOP EDGAR SHAW

6-7) These chosen people of God were told by Him whenever white spots appeared they must be presented to the priest. The priest then would pronounce him unclean. If the white spot in the skin of the flesh, and in the sight be deeper than the skin, and the hair not turning white; then the priest shall shut up him that hath the plague. When Moses' sister, Miriam, talked against Moses, God rebuked her. God then cursed her by putting leprosy on her (Numbers 12:10). Having leprosy was a sin before God, simply because it was one flesh, or one color.

My last point I wish to make in this area is when the Prophet Elisha and his servant Gehazi met with the captain of the Syrian army whose name was Naaman. This captain also had leprosy and requested to be healed. God removed the leprosy and then Naaman offered God's prophet a gift, but he declined it. After seeing Elisha turning down the gift, his servant Gehazi immediately followed after Naaman requesting for the gift himself, wishing for a talent of silver, and two changes of garments. When Gehazi returned to Elisha, Elisha was not pleased with him, because of his scheme. He told Gehazi that the leprosy that Naaman had shall cleave unto him and his seed forever, and he went out from his presence a leper as white as snow (II Kings 5:9-27)

The first man came out of Ethiopia and every man looked the same. The change occurred due to leprosy and the change of region. Now let me point out to you the region. If you recall Noah's three sons and

THE UNTOLD STORY

descendants make up the whole entire world today, which confirmed that man came from the one source, which is Ethiopia. There will be many people that will deny this information simply because of accepting God's word as it is, and making this a complicated issue, which is not. One of the reasons would be self-pride. Self-pride has separated man to this point, as well as racism. Racism is a sin before God. God's purpose for man was to replenish the earth and have dominion over everything until they disobeyed him. Therefore God selected people of his own heart, but they failed also due to disobedience. People are saying why sin is so rapid today; it is simply because man does not wish to follow God's word. II Chronicles 7:14 says, "if my people, which are called by my name, shall humble themselves and pray, and seek my face, and turn from their wicked ways; then will I hear from heaven, and will forgive their sin, and will heal their land.

The changing of man, the Ethiopian

Ham and Shem remained and established the East, while Japheth traveled North. Shem's descendants eventually became God's chosen people (Genesis 9: 26). Abraham was under the line of Shem (Genesis 11: 10-27), originally Ethiopians in territory, now Semites, God's chosen people. As you can see no race or color existed. Ham (Genesis 10:6-7), and his descendants, Ethiopia, Egypt, Libya, and Canaan, Israel Today, also Arabia. God's chosen people lived in Canaan, Ham's son, Canaan's homeland. They in fact spoke the same language which was Hamitic and Semitic. Japheth's descendants were the Greeks, Persia, which currently is Iran, Turkey, Russia, Germany, Pakistan, and all of Europe. Major mutations or changes took place among the descendants of Japheth. This is obvious because of their white skin. In other words, they were black at one time but their skin changed to white. This pattern can be understood in view of the total world population. Over two-thirds of the population of the world consists of colored people. That ratio of 2-1 - two of out Noah's three sons remained black. We know this to be true because of many of the people throughout Africa, Asia, Latin America and the islands in the Pacific Ocean are yellow, brown or black. They have facial features like the Congoid Africans, especially the Vietnamese, Filipinos, the people of India; they are a mixture of black Dravidians and Indo-Europeans, Thailanders, Burmese, Indonesians, Guineans, Sumatrans, and Aborigines of Australia. (Refer to "From Babylon to Timbuktu" by Revered Rudolph R. Windsor.)

The last of Japheth's sons was Tiras, (Genesis 10:2), the father or ancestor of the Thracians. This land, Thrace, was situated north of North Asia Minor and northeast of Greece. Japheth's grandson, Ashkenaz (Genesis 10:3) formed the Germanic race; in the Hebrew language the word means German. The separation of the descendants took place at the Tower of Babel (Genesis 11:9) when God confounded the language; that incident changed the course of history, which caused the human race to speak in different languages as you see today.

THE UNTOLD STORY

By 378 A.D., the Germanic tribes were on the move. They were known under these names: Lombards, Burgundians, franks, Saxons, Anglos, Jutes, Ostrogoths, Visigoths, Suevis, and Vandals. These ten Germanic Barbarian tribes settled all over Western Europe as we know today. All of these tribes were the descendants of Japheth.

The ancient people did not classify races according to skin color, like modern nations of Europe and America. The ancients, including the Greeks and Romans, identified people to their national or tribal names. For example, when God spoke to his prophets Isaiah and Ezekiel, he mentioned to them Japheth's sons (Isaiah 66:19), and in Ezekiel 27:13, Daniel 8: 21 he speaks of Grecia, which is Greece. They used the terms Visigoths, Vandals, Saxons, Ethiopians, Carthagians, Jews, Arabs, Persians, Babylonians, Egyptians, and Moors. They did not use the term. 'Negro', which is a modern term to refer to black races or the world (Caucasian to refer to the White races). Dividing the world along a color line was an idea that originated with the White Supremists in Europe after the Renaissance. The Europeans did not have any great civilization immediately after the fall of Greece and Rome.

Who Started Racism

During the Middle Ages, the black nations of Africa and Asia had the greatest political, economical, educational, and military efficiency in the world. At this time, Europe existed in a state of darkness for a thousand years. In the 17th Century and later, Europe began to emerge out of the slough of ignorance, and certain Germans and others conceived of themselves as belonging to a superior race. Johann F. Blumenbach, a German (1752-1840), was the first to divide humanity on the basis of skin color. Up to this time, no such attempts had been made. His classification set up a color line, to the detriment of later generations. Mr. Blumenbach classified five chief races of mankind: Caucasian, Mongolian, Ethiopian, American (Indians), and Malayan. Moreover, he considered the Caucasian to be the original race. Blumenbach, the anthropologist, named Whites after Caucasus Mountains (these mountains in his thought pattern confirmed the purest white people who have originated from there). Blumenbach was a racist, so was J.A. Gobineau. A third man by the name of H.S. Chamberlain wanted to advance the supremacy of the white Nordic race and its culture. These men attributed psychological value and importance of race. This was racism, which later caused slavery and the persecution of the Jews in Germany. (T.R. Garth wrote in his book, "Race Psychology" (1931), "Any disposition on our part to withhold from some race the right to free and full development must be taken as an indication of rationalization on the account of race prejudice, and such an attitude is inexcusable in an intelligent populace."

Racism has affected many races throughout the world, which has caused much division. Satan is the instigator to it all simply because he is the adversary. Satan's purpose is to kill, steal and destroy lives at any cost. He has specifically used the government, and media to deceive the people of all nationalities. The reason he has been able to deceive is simply because they are of his seed. He will continue to deceive people until God and his Son bring him and his seed to the end. Genesis 3:15, confirms his seed - those that oppose God, his word, and his commandments - every one on this earth was created by God, he established commandments and statutes we must follow. He put the first man in the land of Ethiopia and made open land to travel, a region that man should have remained until Satan again enters and causes man to be scattered throughout the world, all because of man wanting to reach up to heaven, displaying the same arrogance as today.

God made a promise to his people that keep his commandments. There are many people of different faiths that do not believe in the true God. Satan has tricked many people not to side with God and his Son. This has happened due to not knowing history of man (origin). You must first start from the beginning to understand God, and that He is a spirit, a spirit that not only made man, but Satan himself. As time draws near, you must truly consider having a relationship. There are times in life that you will find there is no second chances. There are those who do not believe in eternal life. But I say to you, eternal life exists when man excepts God and his Son. There are some religions and cultures that will not accept the thought of believing

BISHOP EDGAR SHAW

in eternal life. I say to you, read the Bible. God spoke to man. He told man what to do through his prophets and apostles. Remember, Satan does not want you to have a relationship with Him. He knows his time is short, and he is continuing his work as long as he can, to divide people of knowing the truth. I wish that all men and women would come together so that we can be part of everlasting life with Him.

Chapter 12
THERE'S ONLY ONE RELIGION

Man has made up different religions and has formed it to the point to satisfy their own needs. But you must keep in mind. Satan's work is to separate man from God, and to confuse him. God's plan has not been fulfilled in many areas due to Satan. Men have not accepted the true responsibility of giving their life to Jesus. Therefore, Satan becomes more effective and receives more credit than he deserves. Case in point, when the Israelites took their eyes off the Lord, they suffered. They worshipped at times idols, marrying out of their tribes, and displaying unbelief, which all is sin. Satan has constantly attacked the weak. Our strength comes from the Lord, not ourselves. As soon as we begin to realize it, the better off we will be. God put before his chosen people a covenant, a binding contract that could not be broken. This was the preparation of the Redemption plan, or as been recognized as Salvation through him. It became available to the Gentiles when Christ came and gave his life for the world. God's plan was not for just his chosen people, but all people to follow his word, not man's interpretation, but His. Man is constantly being deceived by Satan and leaning to his own understanding, and making his own guidelines and rules, to suit his own purpose. God works on condition, those conditions are: "For God so loved the world, that he gave his only begotten son, that whosoever believeth in him should not perish, but have everlasting life (John 3:16). God's purpose was to bring man back to Him, due to Adam's fall. Man was cursed from the beginning of time (Genesis 3:17) because of disobedience and the adversary Satan deceiving as he is doing today. God has used me to share this important word to you, because his wish is for everyone not to perish. This book is going to open the truth in many areas, and to see that everyone is important in God's sight.

I must now share with you and confirm that there's only one religion. God's word was given to his chosen people, and later to the world. It was written in Hebrew, Aramaic, Greek, and later The King James version. The Catholic Church was identified in Rome, which many churches and denominations spread. The separations of the different denominations have caused confusion. Remember Satan has been a thorn in the just and unjust; his purpose is to destroy. He confuses people to the point to serve gods, or another way by saying idols, which do not answer prayer. Through denominations, the church has not been effective for God, simply

THE UNTOLD STORY

because Satan separates people. Satan never stops. He is working around the clock. For example, look at the world and the many problems that you see, i.e., The trouble that people have on their jobs, their families, and at home. The church is one body of believers that come together, not separated. Until we begin to realize the importance of coming together for one common cause, the less off we will be for the Lord.

The Roman Empire, at the birth of Mohammed, was divided into two parts: The Western Empire with the capital at Rome and the Byzantine Empire with the capital at Constantinople. The Roman Empire in the west collapsed A.D. 476 after many barbarian raids and incursions. The Germanic tribes crossed the borders and penetrated into all the territory of the Western Empire, including Africa. The Eastern Empire was stripped of its vigor by repeated wars with Parthia (Persia). This empire could not maintain its possessions with a firm grip. Constant imposition of heavy taxes, shortage of soldiers, and agricultural laborers, economic exhaustion, a large slave class, and influx of the barbarians with frequent wars brought disorder, and weakened both the Western and Eastern Empires.

With the defeat of the Jewish and Christian power in Arabia, the stage was now set for the rise of a new power on the world seen; this new power was Arabia. The Arabian Empire, with its new religion (Islam) established the super structure of its culture on the ruins of the Roman Empire in the Middle East, Africa,

BISHOP EDGAR SHAW

and parts of Europe. Europe remained inactive for a thousand years (through the Dark Ages) while the Moslem Empire mastered the civilization progressive world. Let us return now to observe the rise of the Moslem religion and empire in Arabia.

When Mohammed was born, many Arabs were still worshipping the sun, stars, spirits, and idols. The Arabs possess three hundred and sixty idols, one for each day of the year. Mohammed was born A.D. 570, four years after the death of Hashem. In his youth, he was never taught to read or write, but his imagination was superb. Mohammed was good in motivating men with the power of words.

After Mohammed became a camel driver, he traveled to remote and intriguing lands. He led his caravans to Persia, Syria, and Egypt, transacting business with merchants of every kind. On his business trips he met Jews, Christians, and members of sects. He questioned them concerning the doctrine of their religions. He resorted to the environment of the Jews and their rabbis, mostly because they were merchants ubiquitous ethnic group. Because he could not read or write, his ears were attentive and keen to everything that the Jews related to him. Mohammed learned and gathered much from the Jewish religion and compounded it with his new religion, Islam.

According to Alvin L. Bertrand, most mass movements pass through four stages or phases to complete a whole cycle; but Eric Hoffer, the longshoreman, theorizes three changes: the vocal stage, the fanatical stage, and the stage of the practical men of action. Mohammed spent many days in the hills outside of Mecca. He was immersed deeply in the deplorable conditions of his people and he wanted to lead them away from moral turpitude and idolatry. It seemed to him that the angel Gabriel appeared, commissioning him to articulate a new religion to substitute for the old. You remember before hand I stated Abraham had a son whose name was Ishmael. Ishmael's sons traveled and settled in parts of Arabia. God told Abraham he would be a Father of many nations. Keep in mind that Ishmael and his descendants were not the chosen seed. Isaac and his descendants, which God gave to them, the only true religion, Judaism.

Mohammed gradually came to believe that he was a prophet, and expounded his religion to members of his family. He went out to the Holy Temple to preach to the multitudes that gathered to worship the idols. With these words, the first phase of the Islamic Revolution began: La ilaha illa Allah, and Mohammed rasul Allah. (There is no god but Allah, and Mohammed is the prophet of Allah.)

Incidentally, by this time the Hebrew Old Testament had been translated into Arabic. The Arabs were rapturously pleased to read about their great ancestors in the story of the Hebrew patriarchs. This fact alone helped Mohammed to inspire in the Arabs the feeling of nationalism and racial pride, because they had read in the Hebrew Scripture that Ishmael was

BISHOP EDGAR SHAW

to become a great nation. Mohammed masterminded the first stage of his revolution by undermining and discrediting prevailing established beliefs and customs and questioning other political, social, and religious institutions.

The prophet Mohammed adopted many principles and laws from the Jewish religion: First of all, the basic idea of monotheism, which is the belief in one God is Shma Israel Adonai Elohenu Adonai ehad (Hear, oh Israel, the Lord our God is one). The Mohammedan slogan is as follows: La ilaha illa Allah, and Mohammed rasul Allah. (There is no God but Allah, and Mohammed is the prophet of Allah.) Mohammed adopted the main details of the Jewish calendar, the Day of the Atonement, the Sabbath, much of the Bible, and many points on the ritual law. The Jews prayed three times a day, facing the city of Jerusalem, and the Moslems (true believers) prayed five times a day facing the city of Mecca.

Trying his best, Mohammed attempted to convert the Jews to his religion, but to no avail. The Jews were adamant and resistant to change. The high regard which the Prophet held for the Jews was transformed into hostility, and rather than allies, he looked upon them as competitors. Mohammed needed the confirmation of the influential Jews to validate his mission, as all upstarts need the backing of someone influential. Mohammed therefore turned against the Jews and became their tormentor.

The offspring of Judaism are Christianity and Islam. Now history was repeating itself. The proponents of Christianity said to the Jews, we accept your Bible, morals and monotheism only, receive from us, Jesus, the great Prophet, the Messiah, of whom all the prophets spoke in the Scriptures. Because the Jews refused, they were despised and hated. I must make a point of the three: only one of the three have full or completion of God's word. God's word did not end in the Old Testament. It was completed starting from Genesis to Revelations. He fulfilled in the New Testament his promise when God spoke to Satan, (Genesis 3:15), confirming that he will put enmity between Satan and the woman. "And between your seed and her seed. He shall bruise your head, and you shall bruise his heel." This scripture is the confirmation that the seed of the woman, would be Jesus Christ. The New Testament (John 1:29) says, "The next day John saw Jesus coming toward him and said "behold the Lamb of God who takes away the sin of the world". This meant that his purpose was to sacrifice his life for the whole world. Now not only that God made a covenant with the Jews, he made a completion of his covenant in the New Testament. This meant that everyone could receive salvation through Him, having a chance to be saved not through the law, but by faith in Him. God's purpose was not to defeat the Roman government, but to secure all people by having faith in Him that they would not receive death no more. He defeated death, read the Gospel of John, Chapter 20. Christianity is the only one of the three that has God's Word in its entirety. The Jews have the Old Testament, not the New Testament. Islam has many parts of the Koran, which was taken out of the Bible. To truly receive everlasting life, all people from different nationalities must accept Jesus Christ to enter into heaven, because he died for the whole world.

Mohammed tried to construct his religion as closely as he could after the Jewish religion. He favored the Jews by accepting many of their laws and traditions. When the Jews refused to be converted, he ordered his followers to stop turning to the Holy City of Jerusalem in prayer but rather to turn to the city of Mecca. He changed the Jewish Yom Kippur (The Day of Atonement or Fast Day), which he had accepted, for the month of Ramadan. Mohammed, the Jewish Sabbath from Saturday to Friday. We have another correlate with Christianity. In the fourth century, the church changed the Sabbath to Sunday and reorganized its calendar to make Easter separate from Passover. Like Christianity, Mohammed included in his bible (The Koran) accusations concerning the Jews. However the Koran glorifies many biblical personalities.

The Second Stage of the Islamic Revolution

The fanatical stage of most revolutions is a cruel, ruthless, bloody, chaotic affair. The throats of men are cut from ear to ear. These is an absence of reason and extreme fanaticism sets in. So it was with Mohammed. He had come to a point of no return. He became a religious extremist in order to give his

THE UNTOLD STORY

people a better life on a rapid scale. Mohammed came to the conclusion that all means of persuasion had been exhausted. The period of patience was past and he was now determined to propagate his religion by the sword. For he said, I, last of the prophets am sent with a sword. The sword is the key to heaven and hell. All who draw it in the name of the faith will be rewarded.

In the year 627 A.D., the Battle of the Foss occurred. The Jewish tribes were conquered by the armies of Mohammed. Seven hundred Jews were gathered in the market place and offered the alternative, "The Koran or the sword." But devout Jews were customary to martyrdom. They did not hesitate to choose. Mohammed carried out his cruel threat, executed the Jews, and women were sold. There was another city northeast of Medina called Chaibar. This city was the headquarters of Jewish power in Arabia. After a long siege, the city yielded to Mohammed. Under the rulership of Omar, the Jews of Chaibar were transported to Syria. Mohammed attacked tribe after tribes and caravan after caravan, as they were going to the city of Mecca. These acts infuriated the Meccans and they equipped a large army to destroy Mohammed. In the ensuing battle Mohammed was almost killed. Finally the prophet marshaled his forces and entered the city of Mecca. The entire city was abandoned because its inhabitants were afraid of Mohammed. He annihilated the idols in Mecca. However he did not demolish the Temple. When the Meccans saw that Mohammed did not destroy their Temple they returned to the city and joined his religion.

The third stage of any revolution is marked by the preservation and continuation of a new order. The successor of Mohammed was Abu Bekr; he was called Caliph. Abu Bekr wrote down the speeches and sermons of Mohammed. By this time, Islam held a firm grip over the lives of the Arabians ("From Babylon to Timbuktu").

Buddhism

Another self-made religion, created by Prince Gautama Siddhartha 563-483 B.C. is Buddhism. This religious leader, known as Buddha, was born at Lumbini in Nepal. At the age of 29, he left his wife, his son, and a life of luxury, to escape from the material burdens of existence. After six years of austerity, he realized that asceticism, like overindulgence, was futile, and he chose the middle way of meditation. The Buddha's teaching consisted of Four Noble Truths: the fact of frustration or suffering has a cause; that it can be ended by following the Noble Eightfold path: right views, right intention, right speech, right action, right livelihood, right effort, right mindfulness, and right concentration (Webster's New World Encyclopedia).

It is clear that the founder of this religion had severe problems from leaving his wife and child. He also was not satisfied being part of or associated with continuing a moral strict life, so he tried the easy route as do many people. He tried meditation. Over a course of history, man has always tried to defuse the importance of following God's way, so they come up with their own idea to compensate their missing void. With their own ideas, they draw others to follow them, causing a major separation in the world of religion. Through his meditation, he formed eight ways to counter problems in life.

I must say, Satan works in man to make him more than he is, and to disrupt the plan by confusing people. Adam and Eve, the first man and woman were deceived to think that they did not have to obey God's commandments, and when they disobeyed God's commandment, man and woman died. That's why we needed a Savior to bring back the relationship that was lost, what we originally had with Him. Everything for men to know is in the Bible. By having belief and faith in Him, and most of all accepting Jesus Christ as your personal Savior, He will answer your prayer. I say, give Him a chance to do that. You will find out that man will let you down, but God and His Son will never let you down. When you are not directed by God, there will always be flaws. God is perfect, anyone that follows Him will be blessed.

I am not writing this book to bash any one, or any specific group. I am here to shed light on truth, and that people can be a part of God forever, not on man's ego, or philosophy, but the truth regardless how much it might hurt.

The Third Of Self-Made Religions - Jehovah's Witnesses

Theology: Jehovah's Witness, member of a religious organization originating in United States in 1872 under Charles Taze Russell (1852-1916). (Webster's New World Encyclopedia)

The Jehovah's Witnesses believe in God. His name is Jehovah and they usually refer to Him as Jehovah-God. They admit that it is better to call Him YAHWEH, the Hebrew personal name of God. They prefer to use Jehovah because it is the most popular rendition of His Name.

The Jehovah's Witnesses deny the deity and personality of the Holy Spirit. They believe that He is a force that God uses to influence men but He is not personal. Further, it is widely known that they deny the equality of the Lord Jesus Christ with God the Father, but they do not even grant an equality of the Holy Spirit with the Son.

I will now point out to you scriptures verifying that God and the Son are one. The Gospel of John, Chapter 1:1-3, "In the beginning was the Word, and the Word was with God, and the Word was God. The Word is Jesus Christ. The writer received the revelation and wrote what he witnessed. He also confirms that the Word was with God and the Word was God confirming that they are the same or one. The second verse confirms that the same or the Word was there from the beginning (Genesis 1:1) In the beginning God created the heaven and the earth.

My second point to this is in Colossians 1:16-17, "For by Him all things were created that are one earth, visible, and invisible, whether thrones or dominions or principalities or powers. All things were created through Him and for Him. And He is before all things, and in Him all things consist.

The Fourth Of The Self-Made Religions

The Seventh-Day Adventists: member of the protestant religious sect of the same name. It originated in the United States in a fervent expectation of Christ's Second Coming, or advent, that swept across New York State following the prophecy of William Miller, that Christ would return on October 22, 1844. There is one consisting factor in this sect, and that is, their constant desire to debate the Mosaic Law, the ten commandments, over the grace of Our Lord and Savior Jesus Christ. God started His plan in the Old Testament. Christ finished it, by sacrificing His life for mankind. More importantly, we fall under grace, which is the love of God, and His Son. He proves it by surrendering His life, to help bring others to Him. My point that I must make is, the New Testament provides great teaching on the subject tradition from the Old Testament. Paul points out on numerous occasions the law. He was what you would call a teacher sound on the Mosaic. He was a Pharisee. He points out in Galatians 3:19, what purpose then does the law serve? It was added because of the transgressions, until the seed should come to whom the promise was made;

BISHOP EDGAR SHAW

Paul is saying the law was the will of God. This could not fulfill God's promise, but through His Son, Jesus Christ, by having faith in Him, we become saved, and that His Spirit is with us. The law could not give spiritual life, but could lead to it by accepting the grace and having faith in Our Lord, giving us eternal life. Therefore we are under grace, not the law. The law is past, grace is present and future. Jesus Christ, verse 23 in the same book, says, but before faith came, we were kept under guard by the (law), kept our faith which would afterward be revealed. Therefore the law was our (tutor) to bring us to Christ, that we might be justified by faith not the law. But after faith has come, we are no longer under a tutor, or the law. Verse 26 says "for you (all) sons of God through faith in Christ Jesus. For as many of you as were baptized into Christ have put on Christ. There is neither Jew nor Greek, there is neither slave nor free; there is neither male nor female; for you are all one in Christ, then you are Abraham's seeds, and heirs according to the promise.

Finally, I have proven the flaws of each religion, which have established something without the complete guidance of God. Heresy had flourished in the early A.D. century, due to Christians of God and their goals to spread the Gospel of Our Lord and Savior. False teachings continue today. Satan is working against anyone that is trying to come to the Lord. He has many ways, through denying anything that is true. Each of these leaders could have had at one point good intentions. But each of them had not any foundation to fully claim God's word entirely or at all

THE UNTOLD STORY

which falls under self-pride. There is only one religion, one God, not two, or three, but one.

We all must serve Him, who placed man in the land of Ethiopia. God told man how to live, but man disobeyed Him and became cursed. Then God prepared a man, a prophet whose name was Moses, who received the ten commandments. These ten commandments told man what he must do, how to live, and not to sin. See Exodus 20:1-17 which confirms that man does not need to do anything but follow His word. Not only did he say follow His word, but He sent His Son for the sin that man committed and paid through Him at the cross, the original sin that Adam and Eve committed (the Fall of man). The sin was removed when He died for the whole world. By having faith and trust in Him, eternal life would be granted. I say again He is our Savior, and that we must accept Him, not man.

To confirm that there is only one religion, God and His Son spoke to John in Revelations 22:18-19 saying "For I testify unto every man that hears the words of the prophecy of this book, if any man shall add unto these things, God shall add unto him the plagues that are written in this book: And if any man shall take away from the words of the book of this prophecy, God shall take away his part out of the book of life, and out of the holy city, and from the things which are written in this book."

Chapter 13
THE SCATTERED LOST TRIBES

As previously mentioned, Ham's son, Canaan, in Genesis 10:6 along with his brothers Cush (Ethiopia), Mizraim (Egypt) and Phut (Libya) all spoke the same language, i.e., Hamitic and Semitic. The people back then were tribes living in the land prior to the Israelites prior to Canaan being established (the homeland of Canaan). However, Ham's disobedience to his father caused Canaan to be cursed (Genesis 9:25).

The notable cultural and commercial cities of these Canaanites were Tyre and Sidon (Zidon), getting its name from Canaan's first born son, Sidon. The Sidonians and the Tyrians were of the same race, and their kings ruled over both cities. The Greeks called the Sidonians, Phoenicians or the land of palm because of the many palm trees found there. However, the

Sidonians called the nation Kenaan (Canaan). This land was located to the north of Palestine along the coast of the Mediterranean Sea. It was bounded by the sea on the west and by the mountain ranges of Lebanon on the east. Tyre and Sidon were founded about 2300 B.C.

The people of these lands were good in philosophy, astronomy, geometry, arithmetic, and navigation. They had good harbours, which enabled them to navigate to far-off lands such as Cyprus, Sardinia, Crete, Rhodes, Cadiz (in Spain), Sicily, Carthage (in north Africa near Tunis), Tangier, Ophir, and the Canary Isles. These Phoenicians were skilled also in metal work, needle work, and embroidery. They extracted dye from shellfish, which were abounding in the adjacent waters. This dye became know later as Tyrain purple. They made glass from the white sand of the Mediterranean coast. The Phoenician and Hebrew, though different dialects, were considered having the same language. The Canaanite tribes that were in this region at that time were the Sidonians, Hittites, Jebusites, Amorites, Girgasites, Hivites, Arkites, Sinites, Arvadites, Zemarites and the Hamathites. Hebrew has its origin in the Canaanite language. When Abraham came from the region of Babylon into the land of Canaan, he found the Canaanite language similar to his own language. It is clear that Abraham adapted very well with the Canaanite language. (Genesis 13:7,12) The Hebrew language was very similar to the Canaanite language says the Bible Dictionary. Phoenician or Canaanite can be classified as an African language, simply because

THE UNTOLD STORY

Ham and Shem are the fathers of the Canaanites and the Hebrews, and that the Canaanites are the blood brothers of the Ethiopians, Egyptians, Nubians, Sudanese and other Africans. In the Book of Amos 9: 7, "Are ye not as children of the Ethiopians unto me, O children of Israel? Saith the Lord. Have not I brought up Israel out of the land of Egypt? And the Philistines from Caphtor, and the Syrians from Kir?" This scripture confirms the kinship of the Ethiopians to the Hebrews (Israelites), which spoke the same language. The Phoenicians established a colony in north Africa called Carthage, and they (The Carthaginians) always considered themselves Canaanites. When Moses led the black Israelites out of Egypt (northeast Africa), Moses died in the wilderness. Then Joshua led the Israelites into the land of Canaan and dispossessed the Canaanites. Now, it is written in a Jewish book called the Babylonian Talmud.

The wealth of Phoenicia (or Carthage) was built on clandestine, technical procedures in manufacture, secret trading posts in the remote areas of Ethiopia. Their knowledge of navigation enabled them to reach the British Isles and the Arctic Ocean.

The English alphabet was derived from two ancient black nations: the Phoenicians-Canaanite alphabet and the Hebrews. The Phoenicians had an effective navy and were a great trading people. When the Phoenicians traded with the Greeks, the Greeks did not have an alphabet. As a result, they adopted the Phoenician alphabet in order to transact business. The Greeks passed this alphabet to the Romans, and the Romans imparted it to the German Anglo-Saxon tribes. Then it was introduced to the British Isles. The first two letters of the Phoenicians and Hebrew alphabet are Aleph and Bet, which is similar to the word alphabet. The Phoenicians also gave a system of weights and measures to the Europeans. The City of Carthage was called the "Queen of the Sea". The Carthaginians controlled the commerce in the Mediterranean Sea.

During the year of 1451 B.C., the Hebrews began the take-over of the land Canaan (Joshua 3:9). After settling in the new land, these Hebrews began to turn away from God. In the book of Jeremiah, God promises that trouble would come, if the Israelites continued in sin. (Jeremiah 1:15,16) "For lo, I will call all the families of the Kingdoms of the north, saith the Lord; and they shall come and they shall set every one his throne at the entering of the gates of Jerusalem, and against them touching all their wickedness, who have forsaken me, and have burned incense unto other gods, and worshipped the works of their own hands". There are a number of prophecies that God gave His prophets. One significant prophecy occurred when the Hebrews were deported to Babylon. Jeremiah 25:11 states, "And this whole land shall be a desolation, and an astonishment; and these nations shall serve the king of Babylon seventy years." The book of Amos (Amos 9:14-15) speaks of an uttered prophecy from God, "And I will again the captivity of my people of Israel, and they shall build the waste cities, and inhabit them; and they shall plant vineyards, and drink the wine

THE UNTOLD STORY

thereof they shall also make gardens, and eat the fruit of. And I will plant them upon their land, and they shall no more be pulled up out of their land, which I have given them, saith the Lord thy God. Joel 3:2 says, I will also gather all nations, and will bring them down into the valley of Jehoshaphat, and will plead with them there for my people and for my heritage Israel, whom they have scattered among the nations, and parted my land. As you can see, God has repeated saying that he would punish his chosen people, for failing to obey him. Finally, when the Persian Empire conquered Babylon in 539 B.C. this also completed seventy-years of captivity of the Hebrews. But now another prophecy had occurred, when Daniel saw a vision. I must remind you that certain prophecies given may be figurative, which at times will take much to pray to understand. Daniel says in his vision, a goat representing Greece and following the demise of Alexander the Great, Daniel 8:20-23, he also witness four kingdoms standing out from Greece. This is the start of the European's dominance. Now after ten thousands of power and 25 dynasties among the Ethiopian, Egyptian kingdoms of the Continent of Africa, and also Asia, which included Babylon, Assyria, and Persia that controlled and established civilization for thousands of years, now for the first time Europe. Before this time, the Europeans did not know about the true God of Heaven, who was the God of the Hebrews. They established Philosophy, some of the great philosophers were Heraclitus 544-483 B.C., Parmenides 510-450 B.C., Socrates 469-399 B.C., Plato 428-347 B.C., and Aristotle 384-322 B.C. One of the generals whose name was Seleucus

I, took over Asia Minor and Syria. Later another king derived from Seleucus I, his name was Antiochus IV Epiphanes 175-164 B.C. He conquered the east and Palestine, which became part of his kingdom. The Greeks have now established themselves as rulers, causing the Hellenistic period from 323 B.C. until 27 B.C. This invasion was the start of the separation and scattering of God's chosen people. Both Greece and Rome was along the Mediterranean, through invasions caused a state of many Hebrews to intermingle due to the control of Greece and Rome. This is how today in Israel the Jews are amalgamate. There was estimated one million original Jews fleeing to North and West Africa. After Rome conquered Greece, Carthage, and Spain, they had full control of the church, and killed Jews and Christians. They destroyed the temple in Jerusalem under Emperor Titus Flavius Sainus Vespasianus A.D. 39-81, a Roman Emperor A.D. 79-81. Rome became rich by conquering North Africa (Carthage), which Rome colonized it after the fall of Hannibal. Rome would not have sustained. Also during the days of Emperor Augustus, he instituted taxation laws (Luke 2:1-3).

During the early Emperors, it was three African Emperors and three African Popes. It is clear during that time, those African emperors and popes had influence throughout the church and government. Keep in mind when Christ was among his disciples, it is clear that his disciples look liked him, and that the government was totally different. There still existed black Hebrews in the land of Palestine that was under

THE UNTOLD STORY

Roman rule; Jesus confirms in the Scriptures (Matt. 10:4-6). Simon, the Canaanite (remember the Hebrews and Canaanites are blood related), and Judas Iscariot, who also betrayed him. These twelve Jesus sent forth, and commanded them, saying "Go not into the way of the Gentiles (Europeans) and into any city of the Samaritans, enter ye not. But go rather to the lost sheep of the house of Israel. This scripture confirms that Israel at that time was a black nation. Jesus points out the Gentiles (Genesis 10:5), and he also mentions the Samaritans, who were mixed of Asiatic and African blood. I must also say that the Apostle Paul ministered to the gentiles, and God spoke to his prophets Isaiah and Ezekiel, that his word would go out to the gentiles. As I mention numerous times and proved that the ancestor of the gentiles were in Japheth, Noah's son. I believe I have proven my point on the scattered lost tribes. Now I will show where these lost tribes are.

During the era of Constantine the Great A.D., 28-337, he presided over the church's first council at Nicaea 325. This council created a European concept. This is when corruption had started in the Catholic Church. The Pope commissioned creating of the gods, faith, man, man as of conquerors. North Africa and Arabia began to notice a weakness in Rome. Eventually, North Africa (the Moors) conquered Spain for over five hundred years, who Rome had previously conquered. The Arabs now had transmitted their culture and enslaved the Africans. The Arabs were the first who institutionalized slavery, while the Europeans made it known internationally. It began when the Pope met with Spain and Portugal (year 1442 A.D.). The Pope sanctioned both countries to take the East, and the other the West. His words were that the African is an infidel or slave, and that he was outside of God's grace. The next challenge came when the British under the leadership of Captain Hawkins, whose ship was named The Good Ship Jesus. This hatred for the chosen people of God from the continent of Africa, has pulverized and scared people for life. The Bible says whatever you sow in this life, either good or bad, you will reap it. Throughout the Catholic Church, there has been much sin. The Jews under Rome suzerainty power, the Jews of Asia and North Africa rebelled A.D. 115. The Jews considered themselves numerous enough to challenge Roman authority in the east and south. Because of their numbers, the Jews almost subdued their adversaries, who had compelled them to suffer many atrocities and indignities. I must now convey how the original Hebrews traveled to different directions. This existence in the Old Testament is quite profound. For example, the Book of Isaiah 11:10-11, "And in that day there shall be a root of Jesse, which shall stand for an ensign of the people; to it shall the Gentiles seek: and his rest shall be glorious. And it shall come to pass in that day, that the Lord shall set his hand again the second time to recover the remnant of his people, which shall be left, from Assyria, and from Egypt, and from Pathros (Upper Egypt), and from Cush (Ethiopia) and from Elam and from Shinar and from Hamath, and from the Islands of the sea". This scripture confirms how that chosen people or detached remnant lived among other countries. I must emphasize

THE UNTOLD STORY

in verse 10; that the Gentiles (Europeans) will seek. The prophet Zephaniah 3:10 says, "from beyond the river of Ethiopia, my suppliants, even the daughter of my dispersed, shall bring mine offering." In the same chapter, verse 19, "Behold, at that time I will undo all that afflict thee: and I will save her that halteth, and gather her that was driven out; and I will get them praise and frame in every land where they have been put to shame. At that time will I bring you again, even in the time that I gather you: for I will make you a name and a praise among all people of the earth, when I turn back your captivity before your eyes, saith the Lord". It is clear that the Hebrews' prophets as well as historians knew that the Hebrews were in Ethiopia and Egypt. Solomon married the daughter of an Egyptian king (I Kings 11:1). It would appear that Solomon established a strong relationship with both Egypt and Ethiopia due to having navy ships in Ezion-geber, (I Kings 9:26), with his relationship with Hiram, King of Tyre (I Kings 9:11) whose servants had knowledge of the sea, along with Solomon's servants and they went to Ophir and gathered gold, four hundred and twenty talents, which is considered to be 12 million dollars, brought it to Solomon.

The king of Egypt, who had taken over the city Gezer and burned it, then gave it to Solomon as a gift due to Solomon, being his son-in-law. Many scholars have presumed that the land of Ophir is on the east coast of Africa (this would be in Ethiopian territory. It could be extremely practicable that Solomon would establish trade colonies along the east and west coast of the Red Sea. Ancient Ethiopia had immoderate gold sediments to satisfy Solomon's need. Solomon's fame traveled (I King 10:4-9). Obviously, when the navy of Solomon came to Ophir, the Queen of Sheba heard about the greatness of Solomon. Josephus the Jewish historian certified the fact that the Queen of Sheba was the Queen of Egypt and Ethiopia. This would signify that the Jewish trade colonies were established in her territory. Josephus also says that the royal city of the Ethiopians was Saba (Sheba-the two words are interchangeable). According to the Ethiopians and the black Jews of this country, the Queen of Sheba gave birth to a son of whom they say Solomon was the father. Furthermore, they say that other black Jews accompanied the Queen back to Ethiopia and Israel today. Solomon's son name was Menilek. Years later, as the story is related, Menilek returned to Jerusalem for his education. On his return trip to Ethiopia, Solomon sent along with him some leading priests and officers. All of these events occurred during the tenth century B.C. This was in all likelihood the first organized Jewish colony in Ethiopia.

In this century, Sheshak, the king of Egypt invaded Palestine (I Kings 14:25). Without doubt, he must have carried away many Jews to Egypt and Ethiopians because he took prisoners with him, and his army consisted of Libyans and Ethiopians. During the late part of the eighth or the early part of the seventh century, the Ethiopians general, Tirhaka invaded Palestine and captured more than a few towns. Even the advance of the mighty Assyrian army would motivate many

THE UNTOLD STORY

Israelites to take refuge in Egypt, Libya, and Ethiopia. Also, God gave instruction to Isaiah, as a sign to walk barefoot and walk naked for three years. This sign confirmed that the Assyrian army would lead away the Egyptian prisoners, and the Ethiopian captives, young and old, naked and barefoot, even with their buttocks uncovered, to the shame of Egypt (Isaiah 20: 3-4). Again the invasions of the powerful army of King Nebuchadrezzar of Babylon in the years of 698-675 B.C. no doubt induced quick and migratory many of Israelites to flee into north and east Africa. In Jeremiah 44:1 confirms how these scattered tribes were in Egypt. Jeremiah also mentions in verse 11-14, that the Israelites would be punished either in Jerusalem and his remnant that's in Egypt. Nebuchadrezzar proves their fate. This forewarning would naturally influence multitudinous Jews to migrate deeper into Ethiopia and the Sahara Desert.

When the time came for the Prophet Zephaniah around 630 B.C., Ethiopia and the bordering lands of Uganda and Kenya were abounding with black Jews. Zephaniah says in Chapter 3:10 from beyond the rivers of Ethiopia my suppliants, even the daughter of my dispersed shall bring mine offering." This verse is a sign that the Israelites would be increasing and main converts among the inhabitants beyond the rivers of Ethiopia. The rivers of Ethiopia; the Atbara River expands from the highlands of modern-day Ethiopia to the Nile; the Blue Nile extends, from the direction of Addis Ababa in a northwestern direction toward the Nile. Approach Uganda and the northern Congo is the

Bahr el Ghazal River. It is estimated 500 miles long, in the southwest Sudan; formed by the confluence of the Bahr el Arab and Jur Rivers in the northwest Upper Nile; it flows east to unite at Late No with the Bahr el Jebel and form the White Nile. ("Babylon to Timbuktu"). These vicinities are beyond the rivers of Ethiopia confirming the scriptures in Zephaniah 3:10, Joseph J. Williams cites a particular point. He said, there can be little doubt but that somewhere in the dim past, probably by the way of Abyssinia, a wave of Hebraic culture penetrated to the Lake District of east Africa." If we may credit the following citations.

Speaking of Uganda to the west of Lake Victoria and northeast of Belgian Congo; it has an organized native government with a tradition of thirty-three kings, and a legendary line that traces back to King David. It is a proud history. The legends tell of the Uganda people crossing the Nile (remember the rivers of Ethiopia) centuries upon centuries ago, and subduing all the tribes whose country they have challenged. They claim the highest civilization in Africa. The one question about the Uganda people would not be their identity, but their validity of the Jewishness of their religion.

Tabiban Kamant and Wasambara Jews

Professor Allen S. Godbey says that the word Tabiban means smiths; he located these Jews in Central Ethiopia. The Tabiban Jews were considered Falashas, but they were forced to accept Christianity

THE UNTOLD STORY

(name only). In fact, they were like the Marrano Jews in Spain, forced to accept a religion against their will. The word Falasha in Amharic, the official language of Ethiopia means immigrants. The Falashas did not call themselves by name; they used the name 'Beth Israel' (the house of Israel), but the Abyssians called them Falashas. Simply because the other tribes in Ethiopia called the house of Israel Falashas or immigrants, this would suggest that perhaps the Falasha Jews came to Abyssinia at a later date. Therefore they were expelled because they did not accept Christianity. The Falashas asserted the monopoly on the skilled trades in Ethiopia; they were leather workers, potters, smiths and masons.

The Kamant Jews were separated into two classes: the Keberti (honored) from these the priests are chosen, and the Yetanti (small or insignificant people). Moreover, these two classes were called by names that are similar to Hebrew. The Kamant Jews esteem Moses highly and many Old Testament personalities; they observe Yom Kippur and the feasts for the dead. Because they remain secluded from other Jews, Christians, and pagans, they learned very little from the external world.

Approximately thirteen hundred miles south of the territory of the Falashas lived by the Wasambara people. They varied in colors from light brown to black. In their land are found asylum institutions (cities of refuge), they are like the Levitical cities found in the Old Testament. Professor Godbey says, "Taken with

BISHOP EDGAR SHAW

the sacrifices, wherever Judaism is acknowledged, they must have been introduced by Yemenite or Himyaritic Jewish traders in very ancient times." In regard to the Wasambara people along the east coast of Africa opposite the island of Zanzibar, we know very little. But it is a known fact among scholars that Jewish merchants from Yemen traded along the coast. It is possible that Jewish colonies were established there at an early date. It is also conceivable that the Jewish tribes migrated from the north. The nation of Ethiopia became influx or crossroads for Hebrew culture and settlements.

Joseph L. Williams quoting Walter Plowden, the British Consul in Abyssinia, after the British Consul reviewed the National Records and traditions he concluded by saying: Two things are certain - that at a later period, six sovereigns of pure Jewish race and faith reigned at Gondar, and that to this day numerous Jews are found throughout the whole Abyssinia. I think it also highly probable that (at whatever period it may be placed) have adopted the Christian faith which they retain today. One other person by the name of Solomon Grazel states in his book, "A History of the Jews" that there still exists 100,000 black Jews in Ethiopia who are not Christians.

After King Abraha of Ethiopia accepted Christianity in the fourth century, A.D., a great change occurred that was disastrous to the existence of the Jews: they became victims of persecution that lasted for many centuries. Ever since the rise of Christianity in Ethiopia,

THE UNTOLD STORY

Judaism has been decreasing. Nevertheless the social pressures and discrimination, 100,000 black Jews been able to survive. This multitude of Jews surviving under belligerent conditions, proves their greater numerical strength earlier in their history.

As I continue to prove my point, it will become clearer to you at when and where were these scattered tribes, which traveled beyond Ethiopia and through the whole continent of Africa, from off the slave ships into Spain, Portugal, Great Britain, and the United States.

Here was another group of Jews, the Jews of the Malagasy Republic. There is an island near the southeastern coast of Africa called Malagasy Republic; the old name for this island was Madacascar. Near the eastern part of this island on the isle of St. Marie, there exists a group of black Jews who called themselves Zafin Ibrahim, descendants of Abraham.

Professor Allen H. Godbey says that the same alphabetic writing that was present in Palestine about 650 B.C. appeared at the same time in Malaysia. Also he says since the Hovas of Madagascar are members of the Malayan family who probably immigrated from Cambodia, this indicates the historical relation with the Jews of Madagascar. Like the Jews of Ethiopia, Uganda and Wasambara, there are a ream of Jewish cultural survivals, complexes, configurations, and traits found functioning among the Jews of Madagascar such as the following: the day counted from sunset to sunset, many fast days, the eating of beef, the New Year festival, the making of a small fire on the first evening of the feast; they have rituals of the purification of people; they sprinkle blood of the New Year's ritual upon the doorposts. The latter ritual could be reminiscent of the Passover ceremony, which is observed in the month of Abiv. This month is the first month of the Jewish Civil New Year. In this month, the kings of Israel were inaugurated (From Babylon to Timbuktu).

The North African Black Jews

In the year 331, Alexander the Great defeated the Persian emperor, Darius at the Battle of Gaugamela, and a new possessor emerged on the world stage and transformed the history of culture of three continents, Africa, Asia, and now Europe (Daniel 8:20-22). Alexander died in the prime of his life at the age of 32 due to debauchery and intoxication. Before his death, his desire was to establish a Eurasian state. His scheme was to combine the Greeks with the Asians. This was implemented by the widespread marriage of his troops with the colored women of the east. Most of the troops subjugated countries, and had become absorbed into the native population. After the death of Alexander, his enormous empire was divided among his generals. Ptolemy received Egypt and Seleucus received Asia. As time elapsed, there was constant war between the two dynasties. By the year 198 B.C., the descendants of General Seleucus had their capital in Syria, just north of Palestine. In this same year, the Seleucid dynasty in Syria compelled Egypt to give up Palestine, the land of the Jews. The king of Syria at this time was

THE UNTOLD STORY

Antiochus III. When Antiochus IV assumed the throne in Syria, (175-163 B.C.), he cogitated the thought of uniting Alexander's empire. This meant the conquest of Egypt. Notwithstanding, the province that bordered on Egypt was Palestine, which stood in his way. At this time, the Jews would not accept Greek culture; after all, Antiochus was determined to Hellenize the Jews at all cost. The army of Antiochus marched into Palestine to support Menelaus, the leader of the pro-Syrian party. As a result, many Jews were killed. Others escaped to the hills and to Egypt. Only those Jews that supported Antiochus' policies remained in Jerusalem. An edict was advertised interdicting the observance of the holidays, the Sabbath, and circumcision. A statue of Juniper was erected in the Holy Temple above the altar. Because of this religious persecution, the legitimate high priest (Onias III) and many other Jews fled into African countries such as Egypt, Ethiopia, and Cyrenaica (Libya). Throughout the last twenty-five hundred years, the prime components that have contributed to social migration of Jews were wars, religious persecution and commerce. All these factors were operating and gave rise to the African Jewish population. In the year 65 B.C. the Roman armies under General Pompey captured Jerusalem. In 70 A.D., General Vespasian and his son, Titus put an end to the Jewish state, with great slaughter. During the period of the military governors of Palestine, many outrages and monstrosities were committed against the residue of the people. During the period from Pompey to Julius, it has been estimated that over 1,000,000 Jews fled into Africa, fleeing from the Roman persecution and slavery. I must say again, Jesus knew the condition of the world; the Jews at that time were expected him to dethrone the Roman Empire, but his only concern was to bare witness of God, and to give up his life for all mankind so that they can take part of receiving everlasting life, through faith in Him. Jesus confirms in Matthew 10:5, "these twelve that Jesus sent forth, and commanded them, saying, Go not into the way of the Gentiles (Europeans) and into any city of the Samaritans (mixed race or Asiatic or African decent) enter ye not. But go rather to the lost sheep of the house of Israel". This scripture confirms that Jesus was speaking to the back Hebrews during that time. Remember that the invasions caused many of the original black Jews to flee and that through intermixing which caused a transformation until this present day.

God's word says, "And the Lord shall scatter thee among all people, from the one end of the earth even unto the other; and there thou shalt serve other gods, which neither thou nor thy fathers have known, even wood and stone (Deut 28:64). This scripture only applies to the black Jews and their descendants that came out of Egypt, who are now scattered throughout the world today. This prophesy and all the residue of prophecies contained in Deuteronomy 25:15-68 passed on to the black Jews after they disobeyed the laws of God. Many nations transported the Jews into slavery, and the sons of Israel transmigrated to every continent. The Jewish philosopher, Philo (about 40 B.C.- 40 A.D.) who lived in Alexander, Egypt, said that one million Jews resided in Libya and Egypt from the Catabathmos to the borders of Ethiopia. Professor A.H. Godbey says that Philo leaves us doubtful about which boundaries of Ethiopia he meant. It is believed as by examining Ethiopia from the time of prophecy of Zephaniah mentioned: "From beyond the rivers of Ethiopia...the daughters of my dispersed." There was a period of over six hundred years between Zephaniah and Philo; which would have pushed through waves of immigrants through out all of Ethiopia and beyond the borders of Ethiopia. E. Schurer wrote that Hebrewism was detectable by its inscriptions from the Egyptian border westward across North Africa to Mauretania. A.H. Godbey says Jerome (340-420 A.D.) one of the four Doctors of the Church) wrote that the Jews were spread from western extremity of Mauretania to India. Now, ancient Mauretania contained part of the territory on the Atlantic Ocean, Morocco, and part of modern Algeria. It is certain that the Jews had migrated all across North Africa by the second century. The Greek historian and geographer, Strabo (63 B.C.-24 A.D.) said concerning the Jews of Cyrene (Libya), "In no time these Jews have gotten into cities, and it is hard to find a place in the habitable earth that has not admitted this tribe of men and is not possessed by it; and it has come to pass that Egypt and Cyrene as having the same governors, and great many other nations, imitate their way of living, maintain great bodies of these Jews in a peculiar manner (privileged status), and grow up to a greater prosperity with them and make use of the same laws with the nation also. In the seventh century, the Jews were threatened with the penalty of slavery if were found practicing Judaism. This cruel policy caused many Jews to flee to the Mediterranean and western coast of Africa. The southernmost point of Spain after you cross the sea leads you to the northern or the western coast of Africa. Throughout the Middle Ages many European governments deported Jews, consequently these black Jews migrated to neighboring countries, Turkey and Africa. The scripture says, "The Lord shall cause thee to be smitten before thine enemies thou shalt go out one way against them and flee seven ways before them; and shalt be removed into all the kingdoms of the earth" (Deut 28:25).

The Penetration of Black Jews in Ghana

During the ancient black empire of Ghana, which was established in western Sudan. At this time the colonial period was instituted, the western Sudan was called French West Africa. The northern boundary of this region is the Sahara Desert; the western and southern border is Lake Chad. Several rivers of this region are the Senegal, the Gambia, the Volta, the Benue, the Logone, and the Niger River. This river flows from the Guinea highlands northeast to the prominent cities of Timbuktu and Gao. Then it makes a sharp turn and flows southeast toward the city of Benin in Nigeria. In ancient times, the Carthaginians from North Africa penetrated the Sahara Desert and the western Sudan during the second and third centuries B.C. According to the researchers of Nahum Slouschz, the tradition of the Jewish traders in the Sahara Desert stretches back to biblical times. Sloushz continued by saying, "And it is not at all surprising to encounter in every part of the desert traces - and even survivals of a primitive Judaism which at one time placed an important role in the whole region of the Sahara from Senegal to the very borders of Somaliland. Between the second and third centuries, the black Jews of Arabia continued migrating across the Red Sea to Ethiopia. The largest migration of Jews transpired during the persecution by the Arabs led by Mohammed. There was a Jewish tribe called Rechab, which crossed the Red Sea and migrated to the uttermost point of the western Sudan. At the same time that the Jews were migrating westward across the Sudan from Ethiopia, they also migrated southward from Libya, Tunisia, Algeria, and Morocco, to the fertile region between the Senegal and Niger Rivers.

The expulsion of the Jews from Spain and Portugal

In the year A.D. 1492, January 2nd, the Moorish stronghold of Granada surrendered to the armies of King Ferdinand and Queen Isabella. For the first time since the year 711, all of Spain was in Christian hands. The decree to expel the Jews from Spain was signed on March 31, in one of the corridors of the great Alhambra, the palace of the Moorish Kings of Granada. The motive given for the expulsion of the Jews was that it was conceived that they corrupted the Marranos (Jews converted to Christianity) by privately encouraging them in disloyalty to Christianity. The ultimatum given to the Jews elapsed Augustus 1, 1492.

BISHOP EDGAR SHAW

Professor Allen H. Godbey says the last Jewish king overrule in Ghana terminated in 1492.

In order to satisfy Queen Isabella of Spain, King Manoel, of Portugal declared a royal ordinance expelling the Jews and Moors from his country in 1496. The Jews who were expelled from Spain and Portugal were scattered throughout the Mediterranean coasts. It is estimated that over 100,000 Jews departed from Spain and Portugal during the persecutions and expulsion. Some of these Jews went to northern and western Africa. These black Jews would innocently go to African countries most of all, because of less persecution and they could semblance themselves easily among blacks. R.H.M. Elwes gives a vivid description of the Portuguese Jew, Baruch, Spinoza, middle-sized, good features, skin somewhat black, black curly hair, long eyebrows of the same color, so that one might know by his looks that he was a descendant from the Portuguese Jews. When the Jews were expelled from Spain, about 100,000 entered Portugal. They were allowed to enter under the condition that they pay the poll tax, with the sense that they would leave the country within eight months. Also at this time, the king beholden himself to take the Jews wherever they desired at the completion of the eight months. When the time elapsed, many Jews were stranded because the king did not provide enough ships in time. All the black Jews who were left behind were deprived of their freedom and sold into slavery. During the reign of King Joao II (or John II), seven hundred black Hebrew children were ruthlessly taken away from their parents

THE UNTOLD STORY

in Portugal and transported to the island of San Thome, off the west coast of Africa. This island is situated near Nigeria, Cameroon, and Gabon. Allen H. Godbey, says that the Portuguese founded the island of San Thome in 1471. The Portuguese were the first Europeans to establish themselves on the west African coast. They came first as merchants and secondly as conquerors and slavers. With the influx of tens of thousands of Black Jews from Spain and Portugal, seeking refuge in African ports, Morocco received a great share. In Morocco there was a revival of Moorish and Jewish science in all areas. The Hebrew academy in Fez competed with the one in Kairuan, Algeria. There were many debates and lectures between the sages and scholars of these schools. Eldad, the Danite, a Hebrew from the Jewish kingdom of Ghana visited these schools in the ninth century.

There are many Jewish tribes and settlements throughout Morocco and the Sahara Desert: The "Ait Moussa or Beni-Moussa, Sons of Moses," is one of the great Jewish tribes. Leo Africanus, a Moorish converted Jew states that the Jews of North Africa are hybrid quality. They have proselytized and inter-married among the Greeks, Vandals, Romans, Spaniards, and Portuguese. The Jews intermarried among the Greeks when latter established their colony in Libya called Cyrenaica; some intermarriages developed between Jews, Romans, and Vandals when the last two invaded North Africa. Before the Jews were expelled from Spain and Portugal there were some intermarriages. Because of this intermingling many Jews of North

BISHOP EDGAR SHAW

Africa still retain much of their colored features. According to Maurice Fishburg (who was quoted by Allen Godbey) he was unable to differentiate a Jew from a Mohammedan while passing along the streets of Algiers, Constantine natives there are seen many Jews of Negroid type. Fishburg visited Africa during the early part of the 20th Century.

I have proven to you how these scattering tribes travel throughout the continent and coastal regions of Africa. I will conclude. The slave ships deported slaves throughout the coastal areas of West Africa, in the Gambia, Senegal, Sierra Leone, Ghana, Nigeria, the grain coast, gold coast, the ivory coast, into the southern portion of Angola, and even traveling as far as Brazil.

God has blessed this continent so richly. But His chosen people of color took their eyes off of Him. God's word continually stand effective to this day. He has proven himself through the scriptures and through history. The Bible is about a chosen people, that first settled in Ethiopia, and eventually traveled to Canaan and became his Hebrews (Israelites) who are now scattered throughout the world. I must give you a quote by Dr. J. L. Wilson, who wrote his history on western Africa. Although the natives of Africa retain these outward rites and ceremonies with the utmost tenacity, they have little or no knowledge of their origin, or the particular object, which they are intended to commemorate. Many of them are performed to shield themselves form some threatened evil, or to secure

THE UNTOLD STORY

some coveted good. But the only reason assigned for observing them is that their ancestors did the same before them. It is written "They have said come and let us cut them off from being a nation; that the name of Israel may be no more in their remembrance." Like the Black Jews in America, some of the Jews of Guinea don't remember their original nationality. This is attributed to various reasons: 1) The fall of the Hebrew kingdoms, 2) the lack of communication with Jewish educational centers, 3) intense persecution and the intentional blotting out the mind their true nationality. Therefore, Nahum Slouschz stated the Islamized Jews he met, in most cases these Hebrews by race and Mussulmen by faith seek to hide their origin, which has become a burden to them. The persecution of the Jews in Portugal was one unscrupulous act that caused tremendous detriment. In one case scenario, Cecil Roth tells us the Jews did not divulge in their children the secret of their religion until they had attained the age of reason. The Hebrew religion is such that if you disclaim your religion, you will eventually deny your nationality. The black Jews came to Africa not only by land but also by sea. In the year 1484, King John of Portugal deported massive numbers of black Jews to the African island of San Thome. The island of San Thome, near Nigeria and the Cameroon, was discovered by the Portuguese in 1471 and it was established as a penal colony. To this island Jews were sent who would not accept baptism. Allen Godbey wrote that Winwoode Reade met blacks in Guinea, West Africa who called themselves Portuguese and claimed descent from Portugal; Reade wrote his book

BISHOP EDGAR SHAW

in 1864. In another instance Daniel P. Mannix wrote that Captain Cutler, a slave trader from Boston, was atrociously murdered with two of his sailors, by a society of black Portuguese established near the mouth of the Sierra Leone River. The Portuguese were the first Europeans to trade on the West African coast, and to establish colonies on a large scale. The Canary Islands were discovered by the Portuguese in the 15th Century; Sierra Leone first sojourned by the Portuguese in 1462. Guinea discovered by Portuguese in 1446; the island of San Thome discovered by Portuguese in 1471, the new inhabitants were black reported here in 1484; black Jews migrated to the Angola coast from San Thome between 1484 and 1499. The white Portuguese missionaries extended to Angola by 1560, but white settlers did not organize a community until 1575. When King Manoel of Portugal in 1496, banishing the Jews from Portugal, all Jews were to be out of Portugal by October 1497. Nevertheless, considering this matter, he decided to Christianize the Jews, fearing the loss of valuable population. He wanted the continued use of their knowledge and services. He stated that the only way the Jews can be accepted in his country was to force them into the Christian faith. In March 1497, a command was declared throughout Portugal for all Hebrew children between four and fourteen years of age to be brought for baptism. All parents who did not bring their children voluntarily had their children taken away violently by the officials and forced into baptism. Cecil Roth wrote: Scenes of indescribable horror were witnessed as they were torn away by the royal bailiffs. The latter did not obey instructions too closely, frequently seizing young people of both sexes up to the age of twenty. In many cases, parents smothered their offspring in their farewell embrace. In others, they threw them into wells in order to save them from the disgrace of apostasy, and killed themselves. Sometimes even old men were dragged to the churches and forcibly baptized by over-zealous fanatics. The black Jews went to Portuguese colonial possessions in western Africa, which were Guinea, San Thome Island, Senegal, Angola and a few islands near the African coast. Throughout the persecutions in Portugal, thousands of Jews left the country. The Jews were leaving the country in massive numbers, that in 1499 and 1531, the kings published a law forbidding the New Christians (black Jews) from leaving Portugal without special permits. Cecil Roth wrote that Christian Jews emigrated to the Portuguese colony of Angola in West Africa were agents of the Inquisition and were sent to hunt them out in 1626. It is certain that many black Jews of Portugal, San Thome, and Angola who became victims of the Inquisition and Portuguese persecution, were sold in the slave trade. This Atlantic slave trade lasted more than 400 years from 1444 to about 1880 in various parts of South America. Some scholars have located black Jews within the whole Niger River bend; the countries in this territory that have contained Black African Jews include the following: Upper Volta, Ivory Coast, Ghana, Toga, Dahomey, and Nigeria.

Joseph Dupuis, concerning the Jews in 1824, says, The land occupied by these people cover a wide extent, between Massina and Kaby. Massina is located in the southern Mali, inside the Niger River bend; and Kaby is found in the southern part of the Ivory Coast. The black Jews of Dahomey, Dr. J. Kreppel reported in 1926 that there existed a large Hebrew community of black Jews in the interior of Dahomey, West Africa. These Hebrews have their own central temple where they sacrificed animals. In their temple are found many laws engraved on tablets which are attached to the temple walls. They have a high priest, with a large number of priestly families, whose members walk from house to house rendering educational and religious instructions to each family of the community.

There are the Yoruba Jews of Nigeria, which these black Jews settled in southern Nigeria who are called the Emo Yo Quaim, or the Strange People, by the native Africans. They called themselves by the Hebrew name B'nai Ephraim or Sons of Ephraim. These Jews claimed that their ancestors immigrated from Morocco. Godbey says this is supported by their language, a mixture of Maghrebi Arabic and local Negro speech. The assertion of these Yoruba Jews is that they traveled through Moslem persecution, until they finally found rest in West Africa. The prophecy been fulfilled which says, "and among these nations shall thou find no ease, neither shall the sole of they foot have rest; but the Lord shall give thee there a trembling heart and failing of eyes and sorrow of mind". These Yoruba Jews lived in the On do district, when Godbey wrote in 1930. This district he says is nine hundred miles southeast of Timbuktu. He also says, they numbered about two thousand people in twenty hamlets. Pertaining to their

THE UNTOLD STORY

Hebrew political structure and culture, they have seven hereditary heads of the community; their leadership is that of a priesthood. They are known to have copies of portions of the Torah (Old Testament) preserved in a most holy place.

Dr. Allen H, Godbey equates through his research, his position that Black Jews were on the West African coast from Senegal to Angola, and they, the Jews were driven to this area from the Central Sudan by Moslems propagandism. Having a knowledge of the black Jews in the United States, Dr. Godbey arrived at this conclusion: These facts have peculiar significance when the presence of Judaism among American Negroes is to be considered. Hundreds of thousands of slaves were brought to America from this Western Africa during the days of the traffic, beginning nearly four hundred years ago. It must be conceived that many Judaized Negroes were among the slaves brought to America. Before Dr. Godbey published his book, "The Lost Tribes a Myth", Rabbi Matthew organized a Hebrew congregation in 1918 and proclaimed that the black people of the United States and the West Indies are the original black Hebrews. With the unveiling of this historical proof and unquestionable who are the original Jews, plus, more importantly the revelation that God gave to His prophets to write or canonical (The books of the Bible) is certain that this message was given to His chosen people who were finally dispersed throughout Africa, the United States, and perhaps the whole world. According to biblical prophecy, the black Hebrews were supposed to have gone into slavery and captivity. The prophet Jeremiah says, "Judah is gone into captivity because of affliction, and because of great servitude; she dwelleth among the heathen, she findeth no rest; all her persecutors overtook her between the straits". As the historical evidences indicate, the black Hebrews were snatched from the west coast of Africa and sold into captivity. Jeremiah again says, "For lo, the days come, saith the Lord; and will cause them to return to the land that I gave to their fathers, and they shall possess it. For it shall come to pass in that day, saith the Lord of hosts, that I will break his yoke from off they neck, and will burst thy bonds and strangers shall no more make him serve. But they (the Hebrews) shall serve the Lord their God, and David their king, whom I will raise up unto them. Therefore, fear thou not, O my servant Jacob, saith the Lord, neither be dismayed, O Israel, for lo, I will save thee from afar, and thy seed from the land of their captivity; none shall make him afraid. For I am with thee, saith the Lord, to save thee; though I make a full end of all nations wither I have scattered thee, yet will I not make a full end of all nations whither I have scattered thee, yet will I not make a full end of thee; but I will correct thee in measure, and will not leave thee altogether unpunished".

The Valley of dry bones spoken by the prophet Ezekiel represents the nations that hold the Black Hebrews under slavery and oppression, and the dry bones represent the black Hebrews. Ezekiel says, Chapter 37, "So I prophesied as he commanded me, and the breath came into them, and they lived, and stood upon their feet, an whole house of Israel; behold they say, our bones are dried, and our hope is lost, we are cut off. Therefore prophesy and say unto them, thus saith the Lord; Behold I will open your graves and cause you to come up out of your graves and bring you into the land of Israel". Meaning that those black Hebrews will return to the land that God had given them. "And ye shall know that I am the Lord when I have opened your graves, O my people, and brought you up out of your graves. And shall put my spirit in you, and ye shall live, and I shall place you in your own land. Then shall ye know that I the Lord have spoken it, and performed it, saith the Lord"? Remember earlier I had mentioned Alexander the Great and his four generals, one of the descendants of the Seleucus whose name was Athichus IV Epiphanes 175-164 B.C. his take-over Palestine caused the expulsion of Black Jews to become scattered throughout the Mediterranean, Africa and now the United States.

Chapter 14
THE LAST PHARAOH

There have been many Pharaohs who have ruled since earlier civilization, starting back with Nimrod who ruled Babylon; men who will try to defy the true God who created heaven and earth. It first began in the east, beginning with Assyria, Egypt, and Persia. These Pharaohs have conquered many countries. The most prominent of them all is Egypt. The word Pharaoh is a Hebrew word for the title maintained by the king of Egypt. I will continue to use this word and to define it as plural. This word was used in the bible either by itself or affixed to the king's name. For example, Pharaoh Hophra (Jeremiah 44:30) comes from two Egyptian words, "per" and "aa". This Egyptian combination initially meant great house, which was the name given to the royal palace in the third and first half of the second millennia B.C. Starting in the reign of Thutmose III (1504-1450 B.C.) in the eighteenth dynasty, per-aa came to refer to the king himself, and from the reign of the twenty-second dynasty ruler Shoshenq I (945-924

B.C.) on, the term can be found, just as in the bible, prefixed to the king's name, Pharaoh Shoshenq. The king of Egypt was considered a god by subjects. He was the embodiment of the royal falcon god Horus, and from the fifth dynasty (ca. 2494-2345 B.C.) on, he was looked upon as the son of the great sun god, Re. When he died, he became the god, Isiris and joined the other divinities in the afterworld. Theoretically, all of the land of Egypt and its products belonged to the pharaoh (See Gen. 47:20) and his word was the law of the law. Throughout most of the third millennium B.C., the king ran the government with the aid of members of the royal family. Toward the end of the third millennium and into the early second millennium, more and more governmental authority became distributed among the nobles and with the rise of the Egyptian empire in the eighteenth dynasty an enormous bureaucracy had to be established to handle the affairs of government. The chief officer in this bureaucracy was the vizier (Egyptian tjaty). The description given in Genesis, Chapters 41-47 of Joseph's obligations under Pharaoh reflects the duties of a vizier. Egyptian kings had five names, two of which were written within the elongated oval loops called cartouches by modern scholars. The second of these two names, Thutmose or Ramesses, is approximately equivalent to our modern family names. The first one was given to him at his enthronement; the throne name for Thutmose III, for example was Menkheperre, "Established is the form of Re (the sun god)."

THE UNTOLD STORY

At least four, conceivably five, pharaohs are mentioned by name in the Old Testament. There are also many other references to unnamed Egyptian kings, a few of whom can be identified with more or less probability. The pharaohs mentioned by name are: 1) Shishak, the 22nd (Libyan) dynasty, King Shoshenq I (945-924 B.C.), who gave asylum to Jeroboam (I Kings 11:40) and later invaded Palestine (I Kings 14:25-26; 2 Chron 12:1-9). 2) Tirhakah, the 25th (Kushite) dynasty; King Taharqa (690-664 B.C.) who is mentioned in 2 Kings 19:9 and Isaiah 37:9 as the King of Ethiopia. 3) Pharaoh Neco the 26th (Saite) dynasty, King Neco II (610-595 B.C.) 4. Pharaoh Hophra, the 26th (Saite dynasty king Waibre 589-570 B.C.) other unnamed Egyptian kings who are prominently mentioned in the bible, the Pharaoh of Joseph, Genesis 12:39-50; The Pharaoh of the Oppression (Exodus 1-2 from 1291-1279 B.C. The Pharaoh of the Exodus, Exodus 5-12 who is identified as Ramesses II (1279-1212 B.C.)

Let's examine the Assyrian kings, or pharaohs. Assyria, one of the major empires in the ancient Near East - The heartland of Assyria lay in what is now northern Iraq around the Upper Tigris River. Its initial development as a territorial state empire came in the second millennium (911- 609 B.C.) The triumphant achievement of Neo-Assyrian was the creation of an empire that went far beyond earlier models to become the largest political configuration the Near East had yet seen. In the first phase (911-824 B.C.), Adad-nirari II, Tukulti-ninurta II, Ashurnasipal II, and Shalmaneser III finally halted the Aramaean attacks that had plagued Assyria for the preceding three centuries and counterattacked through Syria, the best known of their battles occurring at Qarqar in 853 between Shalmaneser and a Syro-Palestinian coalition that included Ahab of Israel (I Kings 22).

The second phase occurred after the death of Shalmaneser III (824) and until 744 B.C. Its first decades saw more military activity against the Aramaeans. With growing sentiment of its northern neighbor, Urartu, and the growing challenge to royal authority by various Assyrian officials. With Assyria and the Armaeans consequently weak, it is no surprise that in the latter years of this phase Israel and Judah were able to expand their territories significantly, under their kings Jeroboam II (2 Kings 14:23-29) and Uzziah (2 Chron. 26 (770-744 B.C.) The third and climactic phase of the Neo-Assyrian period, the century (744-627) of Tiglath-pileser III, Shalmaneser V, Sargon II, Sennacherib, Esarhaddon and Ashurbanipal. Under the standard set by Tiglath-pileser, they restored royal power and established a standing army, whose constant campaigning eventually brought under Assyrian sway almost all of the Near East. The aim now was not simply spoil, but permanent conquest - an empire of a province and vassal states backed by an increased use of deportation to control the conquered. Eventually revolts strained Assyrian resources and organization and exacerbated latent tensions within the ruling elite, which resurfaced in the assassination of Sennacherib (681) and especially in the civil war between Ashurbanipal and his brother, who was a

THE UNTOLD STORY

regent of Babylonia, a constantly troublesome vassal (652-648 B.C.) Ashurbanipal won, but the ensuing military and political exhaustion began a loosening of imperial authority. The process accelerated after the death of Ashurbanipal (627) in the fourth phase and final of Neo-Assyrian history, many subjects openly asserted themselves against Assyria, like Babylon/Chaldean dynasty, the Medes-conflict broke out again among the Assyrians elite for what power remained. Exploiting this conflict, the Medes and Chaldeans began to attack Assyrians' heartland and between 614 and 612, the capital cities fell into their hands. But in 610-609 B.C., a Chaldean army dislodged it, through the help of Josiah of Judah, who at the cost of his life (2 Kings 23:29) delayed the arrival of Egyptian forces. With that, the Assyrians' state disappeared and the bulk of its territories were taken by the Chaldeans.

The next ancient country of the east is Babylon. Babylon in the Hebrew bible is "bavel" and refers to both Babylonia, and Babylon, the region and its capital. Babylon covered over two thousand acres, making it one of the largest ancient Mesopotamian sites. It is located along the Euphrates River in the area where it most closely approaches the Tigris River, in what is now Iraq. Its location at the northern end of Euphrates flood plain gave Babylon potential control of major trade routes. Babylon has supported settled life from as early as the sixth millennium B.C. Babylon is first mentioned during the Sargonic King, Sharkali-sharri (2217-2193 B.C.) By this time, there were already two temples on the site. Under King

BISHOP EDGAR SHAW

Hammurabi (1792-1750 B.C.) the city achieved little notoriety, however, until the nineteenth century B.C. when the Amorites, under Sumu-abum founded their dynasty at Babylon. The previously weak political position of Babylon strengthened during the reign of that city's and dynasty's most famous king, Hammurabi. The influence of Babylon spread to the Palestine region; Hammurabi had ambassadors residing in Hazor. Hammurabi's political keenness and charismatic personality enabled him to unify Babylon. Several generations later, in 1595 B.C., his successors lost the city when the Hittites, under Murshili I sacked Babylon. Babylon did not experience another golden age until the reign of Nabonassar (747-734 B.C.) This period was so significant that the Babylonian Chronicle (a contemporary historical record) began its account with it and later Ptolemic records assign an exact date and time to its beginning. It is a period marked by a curious blend of cultural achievement and political unrest, a time in which the fortunes of the Israelite nation are intertwined with those of Mesopotamia. After King Nabonassar no longer remained king, the kings of Assyria, Tiglath-pileser III, Shalmaneser V, and Sennacherib were in control of Babylon.

The next major contact between Babylon and biblical kings came during the reign of the Babylonian Nebuchadrezzar II (605-562 B.C.) He carried King Jehoiachin of Judah and his family into exile. Records from the palace in Babylon list the portions the Israelite monarch and family received. Nebuchadrezzar installed Jehoiachin's uncle, Zedekiah, as governor of

THE UNTOLD STORY

Jerusalem. When Zedekiah rebelled, Nebuchadrezzar laid siege to the city, destroyed the Temple and carried the remnant of the population off to exile in Babylonia (2 Kings 24:10-25: 21). Political intrigue and domestic unrest plagued Babylonia again. The final Babylonian king, Nabonidus (555-539), exhibited personality flaws severe enough to receive mention in Daniel 4, although they are ascribed to Nebuchadrezzar. Nabonidus absented himself from Babylon at the time of the New Year's Feast, making its observance impossible, sequestered himself for ten years in the Arabian caravan city of Teima. A Qumran fragment speaks of this incident. The weakening of Babylon left the door open for rule by a new, non-Mesopotamian dynasty.

Finally, on the east (Persia) - The Persian or Achaemenid dynasty, of which Cyrus (538-530 B.C.) was the first important ruler, restored not only the fortunes of Babylon, but of the cities and regions Babylon had conquered. In 538, Cyrus granted permission for the Jews exiled in Babylon to return to Jerusalem. Among the Jewish community, Cyrus enjoyed a good reputation. Isaiah called him God's anointed (45:1). Restoration of the Temple was interrupted and not resumed until the reign of Achemenid, King Darius (522-486 B.C.) The rulers of the empire were: Cyrus (560-530) Cambyses (530-522); Darius (522-486); Xerxex I (486-465); Artaxerxes I (465-424) Xerxes II (424) Sogdianos (424-423); Darius II (423-405/4); Artaxerxes II (405/4-359/8); Artaxerxes III (359/58-338/37); Artaxerxes

IV (338/37-336); and Darius III (336-330). Of these, Cyrus is hailed as the chosen deliverer of the Jews from Babylon (Isaiah 44:28, my shepherd; 45:1. The reign of Darius I provides the dating framework for the books of Habakkuk and Zechariah. Artaxerxes is mentioned in Ezra 6:14; 7:1 and 9:9 and in Nehemiah 2:1; 5:14; and 13:6. The story of Esther is set in the reign of Ahasuerus (Xerxes, 1:1-2. A later Darious II or III is named in Neh, 12:22. The territory of the ancient Israelites became part of the Persian Empire when it was established in the sixth century B.C. As part of the Persian Empire, Judah was known as Yahud (Harper's Bible Dictionary).

At this point and time, I will expand on the West. You recall that I presented a question to you regarding the Anti-Christ, whether he would be coming from the East or the West. My answer to that question is the West. God's word and revelation is very definitive. Number one, God has defeated the strong powers of the East, starting with Egypt, Assyria, Babylon and Persia. The only existing powers of this time is the West, which embodies the whole European nations. The two major powers are the United States and Great Britain, plus the associated nations or union. Daniel prophesied of these nations, which represents ten toes. It is clear through history that this same European government will introduce the Anti-Christ to the world. Don't be misled of what's going on in the middle east, or Iraq. These countries cannot dominate the ten nations of the world. God has thwarted the Eastern countries. These countries have fallen. Iraq has been invaded by the United States and Great Britain. Iraq, which was formerly named Babylon, already had fallen somewhere around 539 B.C. The Book of Daniel was written in Aramaic and Hebrew and confirms the historic, prophetic account. Daniel had been exiled along with other Hebrews taken from out of Jerusalem. He spoke in the dialect and wrote in the language that he was in exile. Furthermore, as he wrote in Hebrew, which was a confirmation to the Hebrew nation as a whole, to determine the total understanding of what Daniel witnessed through God's revelation. The book is divinely written by God's servant. Speculation will persist simply because the adversary does not wish for anyone to know the truth. The Books of Daniel and Revelation correspond. Daniel speaks of the kingdoms of the world, starting with Babylon. Mede-Persia, Greece, and Rome. The first three kingdoms are represented by animals, number one, a leopard (Babylon) two, a bear (Mede-Persia), three, a lion (Greece). Daniel's fourth beast (Daniel 7:24) — the ten horns are explained in this book and in Revelation 17:12, to be ten kingdoms. The apostle John picks up where Daniel left off regarding the ten kings, which is the last Gentile world powers, a confederated ten nation kingdom empire covering the sphere of the authority of ancient Rome. Revelations 13:1-3 refers to the ten kingdom empire vs 4-10 to the emperor who is emphatically the Beast. Fragments of the Roman empire have never ceased to exist as separate kingdoms. It was an imperial form of government, which ceased; the one head wounded to death. What we have prophetically in Rev. 13:3 is the restoration of the imperial form as such through over a federated empire of ten kingdoms, the head is healed, restored, there is an emperor again, the beast, Satan has organized the world of unbelieving mankind upon his cosmic principles of force, greed, selfishness, ambition and pleasure. Matt 6:8-9, John 12:31, John 16:3-6, Eph 2:2, 11-12, and John 2:15-17. This world system is imposing and powerful with armies and fleets, is often outwardly religious, scientific, cultural, and elegant; but seething with national and commercial rival and ambitions, is upheld in any real crisis only by armed force and dominated by satanic principles. The Anti-Christ, the person is to be distinguished from the many Anti-Christ (I John 12:18) and the spirit of the Anti-Christ. I John 3:6, the supreme mark of all is the denial of the Christian truth of incarnation of the logos, the eternal Son (John 1:4, Matt. 1:16). The many anti-Christs preceded and prepare the way for the Anti-Christ who is the Beast out of the earth of Rev. 13:2-17 and the false prophet Rev. 16:13, Rev. 20:10). He is the last ecclesiastical head as the Beast of Rev. 13:1-8 is the last civil head.

CONCLUSION

II Thessalonians Chapter 2:3-9, reads, "let no man deceive you by any means, for that day shall not come, except there comes a falling away first, and that man of sin be revealed, the son of perdition. (The falling away simply means people turning away from God, which is currently happening today.) That man of sin is the Anti-Christ, the son of Satan, hell or perdition. Verse 4: Who opposeth and exalteth himself above all that is called God, or that worshipped, so that he as God sitteth in the temple of God, shewing himself that he is God. Remember ye not, that when I was yet with you, I told you these things. And now ye knew what withholdeth that he might be revealed in his time. For this mystery of iniquity doth already work, this verse confirms during Paul's time the Roman government was in power. Sin was in existence. This epistle occurred during or around reign of Titus, who prior assisted his father 66-70 A.D. Titus led the forces that captured Jerusalem and destroyed the temple. In verse 8, and then shall that wicked be revealed, whom

BISHOP EDGAR SHAW

the Lord shall consume with the spirit of his mouth, and shall destroy with the brightness of his coming. Many TV evangelists and some so-called prophets will say that the anti-Christ is coming out of the East, some will say Syria. I beg to differ simply because the Syrian government is not stronger than the European government, nor do they have any strong connections with Israel. There is no comparison between the two. Some have said Babylon. I dismiss that assumption, because Babylon has been defeated by God around 536 B.C. The contention of Babylon or Iraq is because the scripture mentions the name Babylon in Revelation. The scripture is actually saying Babylon was the beginning of sin, and that anyone who adopts the ways of the first Babylon, truly becomes part of the Mother and Harlot. Babylon today, which is currently Iraq, is not even larger than the state of California. In one other revelation, Daniel 2:44-46, the last Pharaoh is the European government. The Bible says and confirms that this is the last pharaoh. It starts out as saying, "and in the days of those kings shall the God of Heaven set up a kingdom which shall never be destroyed; and the kingdom shall not be left to other people, but it shall break in pieces and consume all these kingdoms, and it shall stand forever. Forasmuch as thou sawest that stone was cut out of the mountain without hands and that it brake in pieces, clay which applies to the nations of the world today, that is part of iron (Rome), the brass (Greece), silver (Medes-Persia), and gold (Babylon)". The great God of Heaven has made known this prophecy to the Babylonian king, through his servant Daniel. This will come to pass hereafter, and the dream is certain,

THE UNTOLD STORY

and the interpretation thereof sure. This scripture confirms that God has set up his own kingdom, which will never be destroyed, but he will break in pieces and consume all these kingdoms (without hands). God is a spirit, who does not need hands to build or to demolish. The kingdoms are representative of the past and the present kingdoms. All of these kingdoms have been destroyed, for the exception of the last pharaoh.

EPILOGUE

As time is approaching, this is a time to truly consider who you must serve, whether it may be God and his Son, or man. God is speaking to you and saying, the government and rulership is coming to an end. They have reign for thousands of years. Therefore the curtain is coming down, the door is about to close, and a new chapter will begin for the body of believers who have put their trust in Our Lord and Savior. Many scholars, theologians will abominate what been said due to self-pride and ignorance. This book is written to enlighten the millions of people to know the truth, God's purpose for man, and to dissipate the misrepresentations, that have pulverized this country and its people which are separated through prejudice. The truth has not been given simply because of fear, jealousy, or greed. God created man, and placed him in Africa and that all people were of tribes, not separated in color or race, but region. Man eventually was dispersed throughout the world due to disobedience, causing a change in dialect. These tribes, which make up the entire world today are called Shemites, Hamites, and Japhites. God's promise to them is eternal life through faith and belief in Him and His Son.

NOTES

Chapter 1
For more information on the Sumerian people of Asia and history on Babylon or Babel, Herbert Wendt, read "It Began in Babel", Delta Dell Publishing Company, 1964. Flavius Josephus, refer to: "The Life and Works of Flavius Josephus, Philadelphia: Toronto, The John C. Winston Co., 1957.

Chapter 2
Genesis 2:7-14, Flavius Josephus, refer to "The Life and Works of Flavius Josephus, Philadelphia: Toronto, The John C. Winston Co., 1957.

Chapter 3
Genesis 5:18024, refer to "The Book of Enoch, The Prophet" - manuscripts translated by the late Richard Lawrence.

Chapter 4
Genesis 10:2, Isaiah 66:19, Ezekiel 27:13, refer to "Harper's Bible Dictionary.

Chapter 5
Genesis 25; Genesis 25:13, refer to "Harper's Bible Dictionary"

Chapter 6
Refer to "From Babylon to Timbuktu" by Reverend Rudolph R. Windsor and Allen H. Godbey, (The Indo-European Invasion or Germanic Invasion of Asia). The Greek invasion of the Middle East, the Roman invasion of the Middle East and North Africa.

Chapter 7
Exodus, Chapter 3:1, "The Test of a True Prophet", "The Jubilees", "The Words of Moses", "The Temple Scroll", refer to the "Dead Sea Scrolls - A New Translation" by Michael wise, Martin Abegg, Jr. & Edward Cook.

LIST OF SOURCES

Davidson, Basis, "Africa in History"

Dillard, William LaRue, "Biblical Ancestry Voyage"

Fischel, W.J., "The Jews in the Political and Economic life of Mediaeval Islam", London, 1937

Gaer, Joseph, "How the Great Religions Began", The New American Library, NY and Toronto, 1956

Gibb, H.A.R., "Law and Religion in Islam in Judaism and Christianity" III ed E.I.J., Rosenthal, London, 1938

Gibbon, Edward, "The Decline and Fall of the Roman Empire, Vol II", The Modern Library, NY, 1931

Godbey, Allen H., "The Lost Tribes A Myth", Duke University Press, p.207 Durham, NC 1930

Grayzel, Solomon, "A History of the Jews", 8th ed, The Jewish Publication Society of America, Philadelphia

Lindo, Hiam Elias, "The History of Jews of Spain and Portugal", Wertheimer and Company, London, 1948

Means, M., 'Ethiopia and The Missing Link in African History"

Slouschz, Nahum, "Travels in North Africa", The Jewish Publication Society of America, Philadelphia, 1927 "The Relationship of the Three Religions, Judaism, Christianity, and Islam"

Williams, Joseph, "Hebrewism of West Africa", 2nd ed., The Dial Press, NY, 1931

Windsor, Rudolph, "From Babylon to Timbuktu'

ABOUT THE AUTHOR

Edgar Shaw, is Pastor of Christ Missionary Crusade Fellowship Church, and Bishop of Universal Christian Ministries located in Philadelphia, PA. He is a native of Philadelphia, PA. He was baptized, licensed and ordained in Philadelphia. Bishop Shaw is a true devoted man of God, a visionary man and Entrepreneur.

He received a Honorary Doctorate and Doctor of Philosophy for Biblical Theology from Universal Christian Community Church School in Wilmington Delaware. His Honorary Degree was given for his outstanding work in missionary , through tent meetings and broadcasting.

He is a gifted preacher/teacher who effectively communicates profound biblical truths with a powerful and compelling appeal to the mind of his hearers.

His mission is to spread the gospel Universally, and to help the disenfranchise.

Printed in the United States
20978LVS00001B/259-285